Damon pushed Emma roughly from him

His lips twisted with derision. "Despite all your denials, you're not as immune to me as you would have me believe."

Emma trembled. His kisses had shamed and humiliated her, for she had been unable to hide her feelings. "You're despicable," she said, turning away.

"Oh, surely not," he remarked mockingly. "Merely human. It amused me to shake that pathetic facade you present to the world."

Emma clenched her fists. "May I go?"

"Out of this room, yes. Away from Sainte Dominique, I think not. You have a lot to atone for."

With a sob Emma ran out of the study. She just wanted to hide, away from his taunts and criticisms...and most of all, away from the touch of his hands.

ANNE MATHER
is also the author of these

Harlequin Presents

and these
Harlequin Romances

Many of these titles are available at your local bookseller.

For a free catalogue listing all available Harlequin Romances and Harlequin Presents, send your name and address to:

HARLEQUIN READER SERVICE
1440 South Priest Drive, Tempe, AZ 85281
Canadian address: Stratford, Ontario N5A 6W2

ANNE MATHER

dangerous rhapsody

Harlequin Books

TORONTO • LONDON • LOS ANGELES • AMSTERDAM
SYDNEY • HAMBURG • PARIS • STOCKHOLM • ATHENS • TOKYO

Harlequin Presents edition published August 1977
ISBN 0-373-10202-X

Second printing March 1980.
Third printing July 1981

Original hardcover edition published in 1969
by Mills & Boon Limited

CHAPTER ONE

THE offices of Thorne Chemicals stood in a mews off Cromwell Road. A tall, imposing building of concrete and glass, its many floors reached greedily towards the sky, as though proclaiming by its height its undoubted individuality and prosperity. A uniformed commissionaire patrolled the flight of shallow steps which led up to the wide expanse of glass panelling in which were set the swing doors giving on to the entrance hall. Emma felt sure this worthy individual considered her a more likely candidate for the staff entrance just around the corner, but she gathered together all her small store of confidence, and mounting the steps she pushed open the swing doors and entered the building.

She was immediately conscious of the pile carpet into which her shoes sank luxuriously, and looked across its jade green width to a low, dark reception desk, behind which a striking blonde was seated. Her skilfully darkened eyebrows rose at Emma's entrance, and she seemed surprised at the intrusion. Emma swallowed hard, and crossed the carpet to the desk.

'I have an appointment with Mr. Thorne, for eleven o'clock,' she said.

The blonde consulted her appointments book. 'You are Miss Harding?'

Emma nodded. Now that she was actually here, her knees were starting to feel weak again, and she hoped they would not give out on her. Oh, lord, she thought wildly, why had Johnny had to get her into this *awful* situation?

The blonde was using the inter-communication telephone on the desk, and Emma, coming back to awareness of the present, heard her speaking to Damon Thorne's secretary. There was the usual inter-change of names and appointment times and then the blonde replaced her receiver and turned to Emma.

'Mr. Thorne's secretary is sending someone down to take you up to his suite,' she said, in cool, aloof tones. 'Sit down for a moment, won't you?'

She waved a careless hand in the direction of several comfortable chairs, placed at intervals, and then returned to her perusal of a sheaf of papers which had presumably been her occupation before Emma's arrival.

Emma seated herself nervously on the edge of one of the red and white armchairs, and drew off her gloves meticulously, wondering however she was going to find words to conduct this interview. It was all very well for Johnny, staying blithely out of the way and leaving all the dirty work to her, but even he could have had no idea of the desperate torment of the situation into which he had thrust her, or surely he would have thought before asking her help in so doing shifting the burden of his guilt on to her shoulders.

In his simple reasoning, the fact that Emma had been on more than friendly terms with Damon Thorne several years ago was sufficient to warrant her intervention on his behalf. But neither Johnny, nor in fact anyone else, had ever known the whole story so far as she and Damon Thorne were concerned, and therefore could not know that she was the last person Damon Thorne was likely to grant favours to.

Emma, now, looked round the luxurious entrance hall, saw the line of electrically operated lifts, and wished that whoever Damon Thorne's secretary was sending to, so to speak, 'collect' her, would hurry up and do so. Waiting was agony for her nerves, and she had been terribly nervous to begin with. Why, oh, why had Johnny been stupid enough to get himself into this mess?

She glanced at her watch. She had been waiting a little over ten minutes already. However long was he going to keep her waiting? She looked hopefully towards the receptionist, but she seemed unaware of her existence, and had now transferred her attentions to buffing her nails with an instrument from her manicure case.

Emma sighed. Was this a tactical attempt on Damon Thorne's part to intimidate her? Although he could not be aware of the reasons for her request to see him, had he guessed her appeal was not of an impersonal nature?

The whirring of the lift heralded the arrival of a tall, slim youth, who looked expectantly round the entrance hall, his eyes lighting on Emma's small figure. He advanced towards her, smiling.

'Miss Harding?' he asked, and when Emma nodded and rose hastily to her feet, he said: 'Won't you come this way, please?'

The lift elevated them smoothly to the top floor of the building, where Damon Thorne's suite of offices was situated. In addition to the usual business premises, he had a furnished penthouse apartment on this floor, which he used for the informal entertaining of guests. Emma knew this. She had once been in his apartment, although then she had used the private lift which gave access to the hall of his apartment.

Today, the lift gates opened revealing a long, red-carpeted hall-way, with many doors opening from its wide expanses, and the steady hum of electric typewriters in a nearby room indicated that this was the business side of the floor.

The young man, who had introduced himself in the lift as Jeremy Martin, led Emma along the corridor to the far end, well away from any discordant sounds, and into the comfortable office occupied by Damon Thorne's private secretary, Jennifer Weldon. She had been Damon Thorne's secretary in the London office for over ten years and Emma felt sure she must have recognized her name, as she could not have been unaware of their relationship almost eight years ago when Emma had been given free use of his private line.

'This is Miss Harding,' said Jeremy Martin, as he ushered Emma into the room.

'Thank you, Jeremy,' said Jennifer Weldon, giving the young man a wintry smile, and then, as he withdrew, she rose from behind her desk, and looked carefully at Emma.

'Good morning, Miss Harding,' she said coolly. 'Mr. Thorne will see you now, but I should warn you that he is an extremely busy man while he is in London, and his next appointment is at eleven-fifteen.'

Emma retained a little of her composure. She would not allow this elegant female who was Damon Thorne's secretary to intimidate her as she was obviously trying to do.

'My business with Mr. Thorne should not take very long,' she replied, almost as coolly as the other woman. 'Shall I go in?'

Jennifer Weldon gave a sleek bow of her head, and Emma knocked with trembling fingers on the heavy door leading to Damon Thorne's office.

His deep voice called: 'Come', and Emma went in,

and firmly closed the door in the secretary's face.

She was in a large, businesslike room, with dark blue carpeting, and heavy blue drapes at the wide windows which gave a panoramic view of the city. Set square in the centre of the carpet was a massive mahogany desk, littered with papers and several telephones. A tray of drinks was on a side table, while the walls of the room were lined with bookshelves packed with books, mostly scientific and technical tomes, with polished hide covers and gold lettering.

But it was the man behind the desk, who rose politely at her entrance, to whom Emma's eyes were drawn, as she tried in those first few minutes to assess any changes in his appearance. Seven and a half years was a long time, and she had only seen occasional pictures of him in the papers which did not do him justice.

Damon Thorne was a man in his early forties who looked younger. He was a big man, broad and thick set, with very black hair which was only slightly tinged with grey. His face was strong, rather than handsome, with deep set green eyes, and a full, almost-sensual mouth. Yet he was a man whom women found attractive, without the added allure of his undoubted wealth and position in society.

His eyes had narrowed at her entrance, and his thick blackes lashes veiled the expression hidden in their depths, but his smile was rather cynical and his tone was mocking, as he said:

'Well, well, Emma. It's been a long time.'

Emma twisted her gloves together, and attempted to walk, with some dignity, across the floor towards the desk. To her, he had changed little, and as always she found his personality electrifying.

'Good morning,' she said, omitting to give him a

9

name. She did not really know whether she ought to call him Mr. Thorne, or Damon as she had used to do.

Damon Thorne walked round his desk, and drew out the chair opposite his own, and indicated that she should sit down. Emma did so, afraid that if she did not, her legs might give out under her.

'Can I offer you a drink?' he asked, and when she shook her head: 'Coffee, perhaps?'

'No, thank you. I . . . er . . . you must be wondering why I'm here.' She studied the ovals of her nails intently.

Damon Thorne returned to his seat, but instead of sitting down he reached for a cigar from the box on his desk, and lit it, watching her speculatively as he did so.

'Yes,' he said, at last, when his cigar was lighted and giving off a delicious aroma of Havana tobacco, 'I must admit I am rather curious.'

Emma forced herself to look up at him. 'It's Johnny,' she said flatly. 'He seems rather to have got himself into a mess.'

Damon Thorne seated himself and lay back lazily in his seat, surveying her sardonically. 'Is that so? You mean your brother Johnny, of course.'

'Of course.' Emma nodded.

'Go on.'

Emma sought about for words. To say what she had to say blankly would a complete admission of Johnny's guilt, whereas in actual fact he had been the victim of his own driving compulsion. But how could she convey that to this apparently unsympathetic business tycoon? Damon Thorne, whose companies occupied premises in many of the larger countries of the world, and who had always worked ruthlessly for anything he wished to achieve? He would never understand or condone weakness in any of his staff, and her brother, who worked in the accounts department of this very building, had found his salary inadequate to cover the demands his losses at gambling made.

But this was not the whole pathetic story. Johnny had found a way to borrow money from the company, and for the past six months had supplemented his salary by this method, always hoping for that elusive big win to put things straight. Once embarked upon this course, he had not dared tell his sister, and she would not have known now had it not been for the fact that there was to be an unexpected mid-year audit of the books, and even supposing Johnny had had the money to return, which he had not, there was no time to adjust the accounts to hide his embezzling.

So he had appealed to Emma, and she, knowing that unless something could be done her brother faced a heavy fine or imprisonment, or both, and dismissal from his job, had been forced to agree to speak to Damon Thorne on his behalf.

Her hesitation had not gone unnoticed, and Damon Thorne leaned forward now, and said: 'I suppose your brother's difficulties have nothing to do with the fact that the mid-year audit begins next week.'

Emma's head shot up, and she looked at him squarely, seeing the mockingly amused expression on his dark-tanned face. There was something about his remark that caused Emma to stare at him uncomprehendingly for a moment. There was no surprise on his face, no look of dismay or concern. It was almost as though he knew more about it than she did.

She put a hand up nervously to the swathe of heavy black hair, which curved confidently in towards her neck at shoulder length, and then withdrawing her hand, she looked unseeingly at one of the cream-coloured telephones. Her long lashes veiled her eyes, as she pondered his acute perspicacity, or previous knowledge.

She was aware of him rising from his seat, and crossing to a side table where a percolator of coffee bubbled invitingly. He poured her a cup of coffee, added cream and sugar, and then brought it across to her, setting it down on the desk in front of her.

'Here,' he said unceremoniously. 'You'd better have that, after all. You look as though you could use some.'

'Thank you.' Emma's voice was stiltedly polite. She lifted the coffee cup almost automatically, and sipped some of the delicious liquid.

Damon Thorne seated himself on the edge of his desk quite near her, looking down at her thoughtfully. Then he shrugged, and said:

'All right, Emma. I'll make it easy for you. I know all about brother John's discrepancies in the books.'

Emma's cup clattered into its saucer. '*You do!*' she gasped. 'And you've let me sit here in agony, wondering how on earth I was going to tell you!' Her earlier nervousness was temporarily banished by the wave of pure anger which swept over her.

He smiled derisively. 'Come, come, Emma,' he said smoothly. 'You couldn't blame me for that. After all, whether I know or not is immaterial. The situation remains unchanged.'

He was right, of course, Emma thought wearily. She ought to have guessed that Damon Thorne's senior accountants were hardly likely to have been duped by a very junior member of the staff like Johnny. And rather than tell Johnny, to his face, the discrepancy would be reported higher and higher until Damon Thorne himself heard of it. It must have amused him enormously to have her come here begging for leniency on Johnny's behalf, although as yet she had not mentioned what might happen to her brother.

'So what now?' she asked, trying to keep the tremor out of her voice. His nearness disconcerted her; when he had been around the other side of the wide desk she had managed to fool herself into believing he was merely Johnny's employer, to whom she had come to ask for help. But now that he was here, only inches away from her, all the unforgotten memories of their association came flooding back to her. Had she really once been able to control this strong, powerful man? Had he once held her in his arms and pressed that now-contemptuous mouth to her willing lips? And had she really spent hours alone with him, wrapped in his arms, loving him?

A wave of hot colour swept up her cheeks, and she bent her head hoping he would not notice. Whether he did or otherwise, he refrained from commenting, but said:

'I imagine your presence here denotes your desire to save your brother from a public exposal.' He pressed out the remains of his cigar in the ashtray. 'Why should you suppose I might help *you*?'

'I didn't suppose any such thing,' said Emma tremulously. 'Johnny asked me to see you. I . . . I couldn't refuse. Not when I knew what was at stake.'

'Of course not.' He rose to his feet, and paced round his desk. Dressed in a dark business suit, and a white shirt visible above his waistcoat, he looked like a stranger again. Which was just as well, she thought, breathlessly.

'I should tell you that when I was informed of your brother's embezzlement', Emma winced at the word, 'I knew at once it would only be a matter of time before you asked to see me. Knowing you as I do, or rather perhaps knowing your character as I do, I guessed you would be coerced into something like this. I also know your brother rather well, and his weakness for gambling has not gone unnoticed. It was on the cards that you would be involved, and as you see, I was right.'

Emma shrugged her slim shoulders. 'I should have known better than to appeal to you,' she said quietly. 'After all, you have nothing to thank me for, and I rather think you might enjoy the unpleasantness Johnny is going to have to stand.'

Damon Thorne's fist slammed angrily on the desk. 'Damn you,' he swore furiously, aroused by her quiet dismissal of him. 'You have no cause as yet to make any judgments on me!'

Emma rose to her feet. 'Why? Are you going to help us, after all?' She was sure he was going to say no, and now she didn't care what he said to her. She just wanted to get out of the office as quickly as she could, before her minute store of composure deserted her and she burst into tears. She had tried. Johnny couldn't deny that. And she had failed abysmally.

Damon Thorne came back round the desk, and looked down at her piercingly. 'Yes,' he said forcefully. 'I am going to help you, but at a price.'

Emma's legs gave way, and she sank back down into her chair. Her relief was so great, she did not at first take any notice of his qualification. She sought the clasp of her handbag, and opening it she looked inside for her cigarettes. She felt she needed one.

But before she could take out the packet, he lifted an

onyx cigarette box off his desk and offered it to her. She took a cigarette gratefully, and allowed him to light it with his gold lighter. When she had inhaled deeply, and allowed her nerves to relax a little, the full implication of his words came flooding back to her. She looked up at him, puzzled, and shook her head.

'I . . . I don't understand. Naturally, Johnny will repay every penny of the money he took.'

'The monetary angle of all this is of concern to the accountants, not to me.' His voice was curt.

'But what other price could we pay?' She was baffled.

'Not "we",' he replied softly. '*You*.'

Emma stared at him. Then she got to her feet shakily, and moved away from him involuntarily. For what possible purpose did Damon Thorne want her? Surely, after all this time, he could not still . . .

'No,' he said harshly, as though reading her thoughts. Don't imagine for one moment that I'm even remotely interested in you sexually!'

He said it contemptuously, his mouth twisted, and Emma felt something inside her curl up and die. His eyes flickered appraisingly over her, insolent in their intensity, as though discounting the unknowingly appealing picture she made in her slim-fitting dark green suit, and white blouse. Although she was not a beautiful girl in the strictest sense of the word, her eyes were huge in her small, piquant face, and her mouth was full and generous. It certainly could be said she was more than pretty, she was attractive.

'Then what do you want?' she asked, twisting her gloves. 'I'm a nurse, not a secretary.'

Just at that moment, a telephone pealed on his desk. Reaching forward, he lifted the receiver and said:

'Thorne. What is it?'

He spoke for a moment, it was a technical matter, and Emma took little notice, but then as that call ended, the inter-communication system to one side of his desk buzzed. Swearing softly to himself, he pressed down a button. 'Yes?'

Jennifer Weldon's voice was cool and modulated. 'The secretary is here from the Ministry, sir,' she said. 'His appointment is for eleven-fifteen and it is already eleven-twenty.'

Damon Thorne glanced at the gold watch on his wrist. 'Tell him I'll be another fifteen minutes yet,' he said uncompromisingly.

'But, Mr. Thorne . . .'

'Tell him, Miss Weldon.'

'Yes, sir.'

He flicked up the button again. Emma had composed herself. The initial shock of his decision was wearing off but he still had not told her why he needed *her*.

He looked across at her. 'As you were saying,' he said, smoothly, as though uncaring of the fact that he had just made the minister's secretary wait for personal reasons. 'You're a nurse, and it's in that capacity that I require your services.'

Emma swallowed hard. 'I see.' Although she didn't see at all. Could he possibly be ill? He didn't look ill, but he might be suffering from one of those awful diseases which revealed no noticeable symptoms at the beginning. She felt a trifle sick.

Damon Thorne returned to his own side of the desk and lit another cigar. Then, when Emma refused to sit down again, he said:

'You must know I've been married.'

Emma nodded. Of course she knew. Had he not married Elizabeth Kingsford only weeks after their separation? And had not the knowledge torn her apart?

'Well, I have a daughter, Annabel. She's six and a half.' Emma nodded again. She knew this also. Despite their separation she had sought information about him avidly.

'Something you may not know, something we have not publicized, is the fact that she's blind.' He watched the reactions she gave; the widening of her eyes, the compassionate curve of her mouth. 'When her mother was killed in the car crash, Annabel was with her. Elizabeth was driving too fast, the corner was too sharp, Annabel received a blow on her head, and when she regained consciousness, she couldn't see. It's as simple as that.'

Emma shook her head. 'I'm sorry,' she said inadequately. 'Will she ever see again?'

'Specialists think it may be possible, I haven't their faith.' He spoke heavily. 'In any case, it's too early to tell. She's too young for any major surgery to be performed on her. I wouldn't agree to that.' He shrugged his broad shoulders. 'So that's the problem. The nurse-companion who has been with Annabel eighteen months now, since the time of the crash, is leaving to get married. I need a new companion for the child. I dislike strangers in my home; you, at least, would not be that. Is it agreed?'

Emma felt bewildered. She needed time to think about something like this. To go and live in the same house as Damon Thorne, to see him often, to care for his daughter; it was the last thing she wanted to do. But what choice had she? Either she did this, and saved Johnny imprisonment, or she refused and Johnny would have to take his chances.

17

'I ... I have a job,' she said, prevaricating. 'I'm a staff nurse now. I expected to be a Sister by the end of the year. I don't know what to say.'

He smiled his derisive smile. 'Oh, I think you'll agree,' he said callously. 'After all, if you don't, things are going to be pretty unpleasant for your brother.'

'You're despicable!' she exclaimed hotly, unable to prevent herself.

'Cynical is the word,' he said mockingly. 'And if I am, you have only yourself to thank, haven't you?'

Emma turned away, unable to look at him any longer. He didn't know what he was saying; he didn't know what he was *asking*.

'It seems I have no choice then,' she said, in a low voice. 'I ... I shall have to give my notice in at the hospital. They'll expect a month's notice ...'

'Give them a fortnight,' he said, abruptly. 'I'll pay your salary in lieu of the other two weeks. If there are any complaints refer them to me.'

Emma swung round. 'You think money can buy everything!' she cried angrily.

He shook his head. 'I know it can't,' he said seriously. Then shedding the mood, he continued: 'I don't know why you're behaving so angrily. You ought to be grateful to me. Instead of spending the rest of the winter in this cold climate, you'll be basking in the sun in the Bahamas.'

'The Bahamas!' Emma was astounded.

'Of course. I live there now, didn't you know? Well, perhaps you wouldn't at that. Like Annabel's health, it's not for publication.'

CHAPTER TWO

WHEN Emma returned to the flat which she shared with Johnny, he was waiting for her. Since their parents' death four years ago, they had lived in this small flat near Earl's Court, for their old home had had to be sold, and they had not been left with a great deal of money.

Johnny rose from the couch on which he had been lounging at her entrance, and stared piercingly at her.

'Did you see him? Is he going to let me get away with it? Have you managed to persuade him that it wasn't my fault? What did he say?'

Emma shook her head wearily. 'Johnny,' she exclaimed. 'Let me speak. You want to know so many things all at once. Yes, I saw him. No, you won't have to face a court case . . .'

'Oh, Em, Em darling!' Johnny lifted her bodily into the air and swung her round excitedly. 'I knew you could do it. I just knew it!'

Emma sat down on a chair and lit a cigarette with hands which were not quite steady. Her brain still would not assimilate itself to the proposed change in her circumstances. On top of all her own difficulties there was the added problem of Johnny himself. Although he was twenty-six, a year older than herself, he had always seemed much younger, and it had been Emma who had borne the brunt of of any unpleasantness he had got himself into. To imagine herself leaving him, going to live thousands of miles away from him where she would be unable to see that he ate regularly, that he bought enough clothes that he did not drink too much.

Johnny was also smoking now. He waltzed round the room, holding his cigarette between his teeth. 'Em, you're a marvel!'

Emma sighed. 'You haven't heard everything yet,' she said dryly. 'Even Damon Thorne wants something for his money.'

Johnny halted abruptly. 'What could he possibly want? Apart from his money back, of course.'

'He wants me. At least, he wants my nursing experience. His daughter Annabel requires a nurse-companion. That's his price.'

Johnny shrugged and grimaced. 'Oh, well, that's not so terrible, is it? I mean, working for Thorne you won't be underpaid, will you? I thought at first you meant . . .' He stopped. 'Why the long looks? Nursing for him will be a darn sight easier than slogging away in that hospital of yours.'

Emma stared at him as though seeing him for the first time. 'Honestly, Johnny, you really are the limit! You know perfectly well that I enjoy my work, and I was due for promotion. I don't want to give it all up to go play nanny to a small child. But you don't care about me at all, do you? Just so long as you get away scot free!'

Johnny looked uncomfortable. 'Don't be like that, old girl.'

'Don't call me "old girl",' she cried angrily. 'Anyway, you may not be so pleased with yourself when I tell you that I shall be leaving England. Annabel lives in the Bahamas. Damon Thorne has a house there, on one of the Cays not far from New Providence.'

'What!' Johnny was disturbed now. 'But what about me . . . the flat?'

Because the hospital where Emma worked was close

by the flat, she had been able to spend all her free time there. She was virtually Johnny's housekeeper, and did all the cooking and cleaning, the shopping and mending. She had not minded; since Damon Thorne there had been no men in her life of any consequence, and Johnny had come to rely on her completely.

'I'm sorry,' she said now. 'But that is the price we have to pay. Either I agree to Damon's request, and go out to Sainte Dominique to take charge of Annabel, or you go to prison, it's as simple as that.'

Johnny clenched his fists angrily. 'How typical of *him* to impose conditions,' he exclaimed pettishly.

'Johnny! You were the one to get us into this mess,' replied Emma, unable to prevent herself defending Damon Thorne. After all, his conditions were not exactly stringent.

'I know, I know. You needn't keep reminding me. But it's typical of him that he should do something so utterly despicable so that I suffer whatever happens.'

'Oh, Johnny!'

'Well, it's true, isn't it? Good lord, there are plenty of agencies in London where he could obtain a nurse or companion or whatever he wants with twice as many qualifications as you have for taking care of the kid. How old is she? She can't be more than six. It's positively ludicrous. Why does he want you? Why couldn't he just let me pay the money back and be done with it?'

Emma shook her head. 'I know nothing more than I've told you. I don't know why he wants me, from his attitude I should say he positively despises me.'

'There you are, then. He's merely taking you to spite me.'

Emma sighed. 'Well, whatever his reasons are, we have to accept them. I don't suppose you're prepared to go to prison to spite him, are you?'

Johnny bent his head. 'No,' he grunted disagreeably. 'And how long do you expect to be away? What will I do after you've gone?'

'I don't know, Johnny, I honestly don't know. It worries me just as much as you, believe me.'

'What are the arrangements, then? He decided this pretty quickly, didn't he?'

Emma bit her lip. 'Oh, lord, I forgot to tell you. He already knew what you'd done. He was expecting me.'

'The swine!' swore Johnny furiously. 'I might have known nothing could go on in those offices without his knowing everything about it!'

'Well, it makes no difference really. It saved me a lot of explanations, that's all. We must just accept it.' Emma slipped off her shoes, and then glanced at her watch. 'Gosh, it's almost one. I have to be back on duty at two, and I have my resignation to write out, too.'

Johnny moved about restlessly. 'When do you leave?'

'In a little over two weeks, I believe. His secretary is going to contact me and give me all the details. I suppose I'll have to buy some summer clothes – after all, it may be January here, but it's very warm in the Bahamas all year round.'

Johnny made a disgruntled gesture. 'Just imagine,' he muttered. 'I'm stuck here and you're going to be have the time of your life.'

Emma, who had risen to her feet, swung round on him. Without her shoes she was only a little over five feet in height, but as Johnny was only five feet six himself it was not noticeable. 'You really are the most selfish person I've ever met,' she exclaimed hotly. 'I don't particularly care where I'm going; I wanted to stay here – my friends are here, my work is here. Do you honestly imagine some isolated island, even if it is situated in a marvellous climate, can compensate for the things I'm going to give up? And most of all, how do you think I feel about living in Damon Thorne's household, as a member of his staff, subject to his commands?'

Johnny had the grace to look a little embarrassed at last. 'I suppose it will be pretty grim. After all, the life in Nassau is hardly the life you're going to be leading, is it? I'm sorry, Em. I guess I was a bit callous. I shall just have to get my meals out and take my laundry to the laundromat.'

'Yes,' said Emma slowly. 'So long as you do that. For goodness' sake, don't go around looking like a tramp, just because I'm not here to look after you.'

Johnny grimaced. 'I'm not a complete idiot, you know. But what about my job? Am I still employed, or not?'

'He says you can stay on, although naturally the amount you took will be deducted in weekly instalments from your salary.'

'Naturally,' muttered Johnny glumly. 'Oh, well, that's that, then.'

Emma glanced at him, and then turning away walked into the bathroom. She had to change, and there might just be time to snatch a snack in the hospital canteen before she was back on the ward.

During the next two weeks Emma did not give herself time to dwell on the reasons behind Damon Thorne's demand for her services. Her days were full with her work, and with obtaining the necessary clothes and documents which would take her to Nassau, and at

23

night, if she could not sleep, she took a sleeping pill and refused to consider the consequences.

The staff at the hospital were naturally curious about her sudden resignation, and she had had to let it be known that she was taking up a post with Damon Thorne's household in the Bahamas.

'But, darling,' her friend Joanna Denham had exclaimed, 'didn't you once know him rather well? I mean, his name is certainly familiar. Isn't he that American property millionaire you once ran around with?'

Emma had stifled her embarrassment, and replied airily: 'He's only half-American, actually. His mother was English. And yes, I did used to know him, but not . . . awfully well.'

Their relationship, hers and Damon Thorne's, had been in the days before Joanna came to the hospital. She could only have heard gossip and Emma had no intention of illustrating their association. Instead, she made it sound as though they had merely been acquaintances.

'Well, anyway,' Joanna continued, 'I think you're doing the right thing. Working in a hospital is all very well, but I'd give anything for a bit of sunshine myself.'

Emma had let her resignation sound as though it was her decision, and not the result of coercion. Her one regret was that the Matron of the hospital had had such faith in her, and now it looked as though she was ungrateful for all the Matron had done for her. But it was impossible to explain, without involving Johnny, and after all, this was wholly for his benefit.

The night before she left the hospital, the nurses threw a party for her, and afterwards they went back to the flat for a final nightcap. Apart from Emma and five other nurses, there were two medical students, two housemen, Johnny, and Martin Webster, a friend of his.

They were a noisy crowd, and Emma thought regretfully that it would be a long time before she enjoyed herself so much again. They put on the record player, and danced to records, and teased Emma about the kind of life she was going to have. They all seemed to envy her, and Emma was beginning to think that it might not be so bad after all. Damon Thorne was hardly likely to be around much. He was too restless a man, too concerned with the power of his empire. And it was quite a way from London to Nassau, even in these days of fast travel. It wasn't so far from New York, of course, but she doubted his capacity for finding an island entertaining for long.

She was in the kitchen, making coffee, when the doorbell rang. Johnny went to answer it, thinking it might be one of their neighbours coming to complain about the noise. But instead, Damon Thorne stood on the threshold.

Emma had come to the kitchen door, to see what was going on, and when her eyes met those of Damon Thorne's her heart almost stopped beating.

Johnny stepped back, and shrugged his shoulders. 'Are you coming in, *Mr*. Thorne?' he asked sardonically.

Damon barely glanced at him, but stepped past him into the lounge. His bulk seemed to dominate the room, and the girls and boys stopped dancing and watched him.

'Can I see you for a minute, Emma?' he asked, his eyes surveying the debris of full ashtrays and empty glasses.

Emma bit her lip. 'I ... well ... as you can see,

there's a party going on,' she said awkwardly. 'Couldn't it wait until the morning?'

'I'm afraid not. The kitchen will do.'

He crossed the room, the others stepping back to allow him passage as though it was his right, and Emma grimaced to herself and stood back into the small kitchen. Damon followed her in, and firmly closed the door behind him, leaning back against it. Immediately, they could hear the others begin talking and laughing again, and Emma relaxed a little.

'What do you want?' she asked, untying the apron which she had worn over her orange pleated dress.

Damon's eyes travelled the length of her body, and then returned to rest on her mouth for a moment, unconsciously disturbing Emma's emotions. Despite his age, there was more power and vitality emanating from him than from any of the younger men in the other room, and beside him they seemed almost youthful and unsophisticated and very inexperienced.

Then he shrugged, and drew out his cigar case. 'Actually, I came to assure myself that you were keeping your side of the bargain,' he remarked casually, and in so doing arousing Emma's annoyance. 'Johnny will have told you his mistakes have all been rectified.'

'He hasn't mentioned it,' replied Emma shortly. 'In any case, I have no doubt that you've kept sufficient evidence to implicate him should I do anything to baulk you at this stage.'

'You're so right,' he said mockingly. 'However, I gather this is in the nature of a farewell party. I called round earlier to see you, and when I could get no reply I happened to bump into one of your neighbours who was only too willing to supply me with the details.'

'How convenient for you,' said Emma. 'Well, is that all?'

'Not quite. I'm leaving for Hong Kong in the morning. That's why I'm here tonight. I shan't see you again before you leave. Miss Weldon tells me you have all the necessary literature and you know my cousin Chris will meet you in Nassau.'

'Yes.' Emma's voice was flat.

'Good.' He nodded and straightened. 'Don't look so miserable, Emma. I guarantee you won't find life boring. Sainte Dominique is near enough to New Providence to provide as much entertainment as you could find anywhere in England.'

Emma's eyes flashed angrily. 'You won't accept that I might prefer this cold, dull island, will you?' she exclaimed. 'To me, London is home. I don't want to go to the Caribbean, however glamorous you make it sound.'

He smiled derisively. 'What shows your ignorance of such things,' he remarked lazily. 'In this, as in other matters, Emma, you think you know best. Do you really believe that still?'

Emma's cheeks burned painfully. 'Please go,' she said, in a muffled voice.

'With pleasure,' he nodded, and swung open the door.

After he had gone, Joanna came to Emma's side.

'Is *that* your new employer?' she cried in astonishment.

Emma nodded.

'But, darling, he's marvellous, isn't he? Good lord, if I were in your shoes I'd be whooping for joy. No wonder poor old St. Benedict's had to take a back seat.'

Emma shook her head. 'Oh, Joanna, it's not like that at all . . .'

Joanna looked sceptical. 'My dear, if it's true what they say, that you and he were once like that,' she twisted two fingers together as she spoke, 'then if I were you I'd try my darnedest to get the ball rolling again. After all, darling, you are twenty-five, and most girls are married by then.'

Emma managed a smile. 'I'm a career woman, Joanna. Didn't you know?'

But when she was alone in bed that night Emma found scalding tears rolling treacherously down her cheeks. If only Joanna had known what she was saying; if she were aware of what Emma had turned down. She would never have tormented her by chiding her about her age when seven years ago Emma had had every opportunity for happiness, but had not been able to take it.

CHAPTER THREE

THE arrangements for her flight to Nassau were less than exacting. An afternoon flight to New York brought her down there at four in the afternoon New York time, and a booking had been made for her at an hotel close by the airport where she spent the rest of the afternoon and that night. Then the following morning she flew on to Nassau, arriving there at lunch time.

Most of the passengers on the flight from New York were elderly business men and their wives, on their way to spend a few weeks in the sun, but although they did not know who she was, or her circumstances, they were very kind to Emma, and she was not short of conversation on the flight.

When they landed at New Providence's International Airport, she said good-bye to her new-found acquaintances and emerged from the Customs building alone.

It was a marvellous day, with a clear blue sky overhead, and the white-clad stewards and porters about the airport looked cool and comfortable, which was more than Emma felt. She was still wearing the Donegal tweed suit she had worn when she left England, and apart from changing her blouse that morning she was dressed for a much colder climate. Her llama coat was slung over one arm, and her suitcases had been deposited beside her when she refused the services of a porter.

But, as she looked around her, she could see no one who might conceivably be Damon Thorne's cousin, Chris. If this girl was a relation of Damon's she would most likely resemble him, but there were no dark-haired girls in the vicinity, and only a tall, slim, fair-haired man was standing watching her speculatively.

Becoming embarrassed by his scrutiny, Emma turned away, wondering whether she ought to report to the information desk that she was going for a cup of coffee and would they contact her if anyone came looking for her. There was no point in her taking a taxi into the city; she had no idea where she should go.

Lifting her cases, she turned towards the airport buildings again, but the man suddenly came to life, and walked swiftly towards her. As he approached, Emma wondered who he could be. Dressed in a lightweight tropical suit of a beige material, his almost silvery hair lifting slightly in the faint breeze, he looked about thirty, and was certainly very attractive.

Reaching her, he said: 'I'm sorry if you were beginning to resent the appraisal, but I've finally decided you must be Emma Harding, am I right?'

Emma stared at him in relief. 'Yes, I'm Emma Harding. Have you come to meet me?' At his nod she continued, 'Oh, thank goodness. I was half afraid ... Mr. Thorne's cousin had forgotten all about me.' She hesitated only a moment over his name.

He grinned. 'Didn't Damon tell you I should meet you? I mean, I thought at first you couldn't be the girl I was waiting for simply because you never gave me half a glance.'

Emma smiled. 'Are you Chris Thorne?'

'Of course.'

She laughed. 'I don't know why, I was expecting a girl. You know, "Chris" being short for Christine.'

He took her cases, and started to walk across to where a low slung white sports car was parked. 'It's also short for Christopher,' he said, slinging her cases on to the back seat, and helping her into the car. 'And you're not quite what I expected, either. You're much younger, and much more attractive.'

Emma blushed. 'Why, thank you,' she said, sliding into her seat. 'I feel better already.'

The drive to Nassau, with Christopher Thorne, was a memorable experience. He took the coast road, giving her the full benefit of the magnificent scenery. Emma thought she would never be able to describe the place to Johnny, and Joanna, back home, without sounding exactly like a travel brochure. But despite her assertions that the Bahamas held no appeal for her, she was unable to prevent a thrill of purely physical anticipation when she saw the fabulous pink-tinged beaches and creaming coastline. The names of the beaches were inviting too; Love Beach, Paradise Beach; Emma shivered expectantly.

Christopher Thorne glanced at her and indicated a famous golf course on their right. 'There's plenty to do,' he said lazily. 'Swimming, water-skiing, skin-diving. Can you swim?'

'Oh yes, but I'm afraid the other two things you mentioned I've never tried.'

'You will,' he remarked, smiling. 'I'll teach you myself.'

Nassau was teeming with people at this time of day, but Christopher managed to ease his way between the swarms of cyclists, the taxis and the horse-drawn Surreys to swing into the forecourt of a huge hotel. The building was all white, with lots of windows with jalousies, and balconies overlooking the whole of Nassau. Christopher handed the car-keys to a waiting attendant, and then called the boy to take in Emma's cases.

He helped Emma out, and said: 'Come on, your room is booked. I guess you could use a shower and a change of clothes.'

'Could I not!' exclaimed Emma, nodding, and preceded him into the hotel.

She left Christopher downstairs and went up in the lift with one of the boys who conducted her to her room. It was a magnificent place with modern Swedish-designed furniture and cream and green walls and coverings. Adjoining it was a bathroom for her own personal use, and she wondered why Christopher had gone to the trouble of booking her a room like this when they would be leaving after lunch for Sainte Dominique.

She bathed in the deep step-in bath, towelled herself dry, and then sought about in her cases for a change of underwear. Finally she donned a pale blue shift of thin Tricel jersey which outlined the rounded curves of her slim figure. She ran a comb through her thick, silky hair which swung against her shoulders and a coral lipstick completed her toilet.

Feeling more ready to face the world, she went downstairs again. It was after one o'clock, and she was feeling quite hungry. To her relief, Christopher was waiting in the foyer, and came to meet her eagerly as she emerged from the lift.

'Come on,' he said, grinning appreciatively. 'I'm starving!'

'So am I,' replied Emma, and allowed his fingers to link with hers as they walked through to the restaurant.

Their table, which Christopher had reserved earlier, was situated on a terrace overlooking the harbour. They had Martinis first and then Emma allowed Christopher to choose what they would eat. They ate fresh melon, followed by shellfish and green salad and french fried potatoes, and completed the meal with a fruit salad and fresh cream topped with nuts. Coffee was of the continental variety, and Emma had two cups.

She leaned back, replete, and accepted a cigarette from Christopher. When he had lighted hers, and his own, he said: 'You enjoyed that?'

'You know I did.' She smiled. 'Did I seem to have an enormous appetite?'

He laughed, and shook his head. 'No. I like to see a girl enjoy her food, instead of only picking at things which aren't fattening. I should say you had no worries on that score.'

'Not at the moment, although I'm afraid this life won't be so demanding as my work at the hospital, and I may find myself putting on a couple of inches here and there. I shall have to be careful.' She smiled.

'What did you do in England? I mean, I know you were a nurse, but what were your hobbies? Did you go out a lot?'

Emma shook her head. 'No. Not really. I attended lectures sometimes, and I enjoy the occasional visit to the theatre. I like concerts, most kinds of music, and I adore reading.'

Christopher looked interested. 'Do you now? And what do you like to read?'

She shrugged. 'Most anything. I enjoy thrillers, romances, really anything that holds my interest.'

'Have you heard of Christmas Holly?'

'Christmas Holly.' Emma frowned. 'Of course, he's that private investigator Michael Jeffries writes about.' She laughed. 'They're rather good. I think I've read two or three of them.'

Christopher grinned at her. 'Two or three!' he exclaimed mockingly. 'I've written twenty-seven, I'll have you know!'

Emma was astonished. 'You're Michael Jeffries!' She drew on her cigarette incredulously. 'How marvellous! Imagine meeting Christmas Holly's inventor. What a wonderful name, by the way. Wherever did you think of it?'

'Well, Christmas is not so very different from Christopher, and Holly has thorns. Rather corny, isn't it, but at least it goes together. And my full name is Christopher Michael Jeffrey Thorne, so that explains the rest.'

'Well, anyway, I think this is terrific,' said Emma enthusiastically. 'Writing after all is the necessary forerunner to reading, and I've never met a writer before. Do you live on Sainte Dominique?'

'No,' he shook his head, and she looked disappointed.

'I live on Sainte Catherine, which is quite close by. Only a couple of miles from Sainte Dominique actually, so we'll be near neighbours. It will be a change to have someone to talk to who is interested in my work.'

'That's good,' Emma smiled. 'Who lives on Sainte Dominique – apart from Annabel, of course?'

He shrugged. 'Well, there's Tansy, she's Annabel's old nanny. I think you'll like her. She used to be Damon's nanny years ago. Then there's the other servants, of course. And Louisa Meredith, she's Annabel's governess.'

Emma was astounded. 'But surely, if Annabel has a nanny, and a governess, she doesn't need me!'

Christopher looked thoughtful. 'I wouldn't say that,' he replied, shaking his head. 'Tansy is too old to take a six-year-old very far, particularly one in Annabel's condition. As for Louisa – well, she's a bit useless. Oh, she teaches Annabel to read in Braille, and she has conversations with her. I suppose Annabel is learning quite a lot, but as far as being a companion to the child is concerned, she's no help. To talk to a child, one has to treat them as equals, not talk down to them. Louisa could never forget herself sufficiently to romp with the child. She's far too reserved.'

'I see.' Emma sighed. 'Who has been looking after Annabel?'

'Brenda Lawson. She was a woman in her thirties. She's married a retired American businessman who has decided to make his home in Spanish Wells.' He rose to his feet. 'Are you ready?'

Emma nodded, and allowed him to help her to her feet, and walked with him out of the restaurant. In the entrance hall of the hotel, he paused.

'How is your room?'

'It's fine.' Emma frowned. 'Are we staying overnight?'

Christopher grinned. 'That was the idea. Do you mind?'

'That's not the point, surely,' exclaimed Emma, involuntarily. 'I mean, I understood from my instructions that we were leaving for Sainte Dominique after lunch.'

'Damon's instructions,' remarked Christopher dryly. 'Look, he may be the big man back in England and the States, but here he's just my cousin, and I say what goes. Don't you want to stay?'

'Well, of course my feelings are immaterial,' Emma said, sighing. It was very flattering to know that this attractive man should be enjoying her company, but she couldn't help but feel that Damon would be furious if he knew.

Christopher was beginning to look a little annoyed. 'Okay,' he said. 'You decide.'

Emma bent her head. 'Please,' she said, 'I don't want to cause any trouble.'

'All right, we stay. Good heavens, girl, no one's going to tick you off here. You're not in your hospital now, you know. Life proceeds at a much more sensible pace here. Besides, I want to show you the island. New Providence is quite a place.'

And so it was. Emma soon forgot her anxiety in the pure enjoyment of the places Christopher took her to see. He insisted she brought her swim suit with her, and afterwards she was glad she had.

First of all they explored Nassau itself. Christopher showed her the Straw Market, and provided her with a huge straw hat to shade her eyes. He bought himself a straw hat, too, but his was much more conservative in design and she laughed when he tilted it extravagantly and did an impression of Maurice Chevalier.

Bay Street provided them with plenty of window shopping, but they did not buy anything. Emma had no desire to arrive on Sainte Dominique already loaded with gifts to take back home.

In the harbour, boats of every kind were moored, from small sailing vessels used for fishing, to sleek catamarans gleaming with chrome and white paint-work.

They hired a Surrey and toured the city in true tourist style, the sleepy back streets a reminder of days when pirates swaggered through the town. Emma could hardly believe some of the anecdotes Christopher related to her, but the island's history interested her so much that she determined she would buy some books about it at the first opportunity.

Afterwards they sought the beach, and the creamy warmth of the blue-flecked waters. Emma had never bathed in a sea so warm, or so inviting, and she was tempted to stay in the water for the rest of the afternoon. But Christopher teased her mercilessly by continually ducking her, so that at last she walked up the beach with him and lay back on the towels he had provided. Her straw hat shaded her eyes, and she felt wonderfully content. She could almost believe she was here of her own volition, and not because Damon Thorne had given her no other choice.

Christopher was a very good companion. His literary background had provided him with the gift of creating interest out of the simplest things, and his knowledge of the area was extensive. He had travelled throughout the Caribbean, and knew Jamaica and Trinidad very well indeed.

Emma was a born listener, and lay on her stomach now looking down at him as he told her about the slaves who had come to the West Indies.

'Poor devils,' he said, his eyes half closed against the glare. 'They left one sort of slavery for another. At least in the southern States they could be assured of food and shelter. Some of them were hard pushed to stay alive here in the beginning.' He sighed. 'And the white population in those days considered the Africans a people who required leadership and discipline to survive. They wouldn't believe they were capable of providing for themselves.'

Emma made a move with her lips. 'I'm surprised you don't write about the islands. Your books are always set in the States.'

Christopher grinned and propped himself up on his elbows, so that his face was only inches from her own.

'Tactics, honey, tactics,' he said cheerfully. 'My books sell very well in the States, and as it's my bread and butter, who am I to disappoint my fans?'

'Mercenary creature!' Emma wrinkled her nose at him, and then lay back again. It was very warm, and she was feeling quite drowsy.

Christopher looked down at her now. 'Aren't you glad we didn't go back to Sainte Dominique today?' he asked.

Emma opened her eyes. 'If you mean am I enjoying myself, you know the answer is "yes",' she replied comfortably. 'But I have a distinct feeling of guilt every time I really consider it.'

He grimaced. 'Well, don't have. Nobody expects us. I told Annabel I wouldn't be back today.'

'Did you indeed?' Emma was indignant. 'Were you so sure your charm would work, whatever I turned out to be?'

He grinned. 'Honey, if you'd turned out to be another Louisa Meredith, we most definitely would have returned today.'

Emma smiled. 'Oh, well, I suppose one day more or less won't make much difference.'

They went back to the hotel soon after six. Christopher informed her that his room was on the floor below, and that he would meet her in the bar for a drink before dinner.

Emma showered, changed into a sleeveless coral chiffon gown which she had made herself for a dance before Christmas, smoothed her dark hair and descended the stairs in high-heeled white sandals. She was glad she had brought the dress with her. Christopher was wearing a white dinner jacket and he looked approvingly at her as she came in.

'Did I tell you that I like the way you dress?' he asked, as she sipped a glass of some strange concoction which he had provided, the top of which was covered with various slices of different fruit.

She looked at him over the rim. 'Mr. Thorne, you're flirting again!'

'No, I'm not. I mean it.' He grinned. 'And the name's Chris, in case you forget.'

'I haven't forgotten,' she replied, and accepted a cigarette. 'It's been a wonderful day. Thank you.'

'Don't thank me, I should be thanking you,' he returned. 'No matter what you may think, I don't find every woman I meet as attractive as you, Emma.'

'Thank you, again.' Emma glanced away, not wanting him to think she had any intentions of considering this a serious declaration. No matter how likeable he was, and he was indeed very likeable, Emma knew she could never become closely associated with any relation of Damon's.

After dinner, there was dancing in the ballroom to a rhythmic all-Negro band. The music was streamlined and seductive, and no one could have failed to find their pulses moved by the beat.

Emma danced with Christopher several times, and twice two older men approached her and she danced with them, much to Christopher's annoyance. But she had to admit she liked dancing with him best for he was a good dancer, and his hands were cool and not hot and sweaty. He held her close, and she could feel his breath on her neck and the faint odour of his after-shave lotion was pleasant to her nose.

'You dance well,' he said once, looking down at her.

'Well, it's not from practice,' she said, smiling. 'I

don't attend many dances back home.'

Patently, he didn't believe her, and she wondered what he would say if she told him the truth about her relationship with Damon. Obviously their association had been forgotten by his family. After all, they had never met her; she was only a name to them, and that was a long time ago.

At eleven-thirty they stood on the terrace in the light from the hall behind them. It was a wonderful evening. The moon hung crazily in a sky as blue as sapphire velvet, while Emma thought she had never seen so many stars.

'Let's take a Surrey and tour the town at night,' said Christopher, turning towards her eagerly.

Emma hesitated, and then shook her head. 'I don't think we'd better. It's getting late, and tomorrow is going to be quite a day for me. I think I'll go to bed, if you don't mind.'

Christopher pulled a face. 'Aw, Emma, that means you're going whether I mind or not.' He shrugged, and then capitulated. 'All right. I'll take you to your room.'

'That's not necessary,' she replied.

'I know it's not. But I'm going to do it all the same,' he retorted.

In the elevator, he smiled at her expression. 'Don't worry. I don't expect to come in. I just want to see you get there safely. There might be some dubious types roaming the corridors.'

Emma giggled. 'Honestly, Chris!'

At her door, he put a hand on either side of her as she leant against the doorpost. 'You have enjoyed yourself, haven't you?'

'Enormously,' nodded Emma, smiling.

'Good. Good night, Emma.' He bent his head and put his mouth to hers. The touch of his lips was cool and pleasant, and Emma responded almost involuntarily. His mouth hardened, and then he drew back. He was breathing rather faster, and he looked a little pale. 'I'll go,' he murmured huskily, and squeezing her fingers he walked away along the corridor.

Emma watched him go feeling a pleasant sensation of tiredness combined with a kind of contentment. Her first day in the islands had been a memorable one. Christopher was one of the nicest men she had ever met, and she might, she just might, be going to enjoy her stay here.

CHAPTER FOUR

SAINTE DOMINIQUE'S bay was a small, peaceful island, situated on the Windward side of the Abaco Cays. That morning, as their launch cruised its way towards their destination, Emma had seen dozens of tiny islands and atolls, sprouting out of the sea. She had spent the journey leaning on the rail enthralled with her surroundings. Some of the islands were covered with houses and resembled villages set in water instead of amongst fields. Others were quite deserted, their white beaches seemingly untrodden by human foot.

It was another wonderfully clear day, and the early morning mist had dissipated leaving a vista of blue sea and sky as far as the eye could see. Now that she was nearing her destination, Emma was beginning to feel twinges of nervousness. It was all very well for Chris to aver that she would receive a very warm welcome, but he was not going to be staying, he would be returning to Sainte Catherine almost immediately, and she would be left alone with strangers.

The launch could not go right in because of the shallowness of the water, so Christopher and the boatman, a dark-skinned Negro, pulled on thigh-length waders and Christopher carried Emma up on to the sand. The boatman brought her cases, and Christopher took charge of them.

'Come on,' he said. 'This way. I should have thought the reliable Miss Meredith would have had Annabel on the beach to meet you.'

Emma sighed, and followed him up the incline and

through a belt of palm trees. They came upon a clearing through the trees where several thatched huts indicated that this was the native village, where the servants who worked at the house were housed.

Beyond the village, another clump of trees hid the homestead itself.

Damon Thorne's house was low and modern, without having the type of structure which would be out of place on an island like this. Shutters were bolted back from windows which stood wide to the morning air, while climbing plants in a glory of colour overhung the walls. The gardens in front of the house were a riot of colour also, and Emma recognized oleanders and hibiscus, as well as more common varieties such as roses and nasturtiums. Wide, shallow steps led up to white double doors which at present were standing open, and Christopher glanced at Emma to make sure she was behind him before mounting the steps and waiting for her by the door.

'Go on,' he said, prodding her into the hall. 'No one's going to bite you.'

The hall was cool with a tiled floor and white panelled walls. Doors led off to the various regions of the house while a horseshoe staircase drew attention to a white-balustraded gallery.

Immediately at their entrance, a tall, slim woman came walking towards them down this beautiful staircase, her eyes cool and aloof, appraising Emma.

Christopher stood down Emma's suitcases, and grinned. 'Well, well! If it isn't the inestimable Louisa, herself. How are you, my old love?'

Louisa Meredith ignored him, and came towards Emma. 'You must be Miss Harding,' she said coldly. 'You were expected yesterday.'

43

Emma flushed, disconcerted. 'Oh, but I understood ... I mean ... Mr. Thorne seemed to think ...' She faltered. Then she stiffened her shoulders. 'You are Annabel's governess, are you not?'

The woman nodded faintly. 'It is obvious *Mr.* Thorne was thinking only of himself. Unfortunately, his action had unexpected consequences.'

Emma stared at her. 'In what way?'

'The nurse who had charge of Annabel left three days ago. Yesterday, with no one to entertain her, Annabel went exploring alone. Unfortunately, she fell in the swimming pool; she can't swim. Had Henri, one of the servants, not been nearby, she would have drowned.' She spoke the words in a hard, unfeeling voice, as though she was discussing the weather, and Emma was terribly shocked.

She did not know what to say. She shook her head. 'I'm very sorry,' she said, glancing at Christopher, who grunted unintelligibly.

'When did this happen?' he asked.

'Yesterday afternoon. As I said, fortunately Henri was passing by, and heard her cries. We thought we had better keep her in bed today, to avoid any ill effects.'

Christopher grimaced at her. 'And what were you doing at the time? Polishing your nails?'

'That remark was uncalled-for!' exclaimed Louisa angrily. Although she was only in her thirties she seemed much older, and Emma thought glumly that she had indeed made an inauspicious start to her duties.

'Well, anyway,' said Christopher, shrugging, 'Emma wouldn't have arrived much before tea-time if we had come yesterday, so you can hardly consider her to blame.'

'Did I say I was blaming Miss Harding?'

'You implied it. Oh, well, shut up about it. Where is the kid? I may as well see her before I leave.' He walked towards the stairs. 'Come on, Emma, I'll introduce you. Leave your cases. Louisa, get someone to take the cases to Emma's room. If you tell me where she's sleeping, I'll show her that too.'

'I'm not the housekeeper here,' retorted Louisa, turning away.

Christopher compressed his lips. 'No, ma'am, you're not. But either you do as I say, or I'll personally make it my business to report you to Mr. Thorne.'

Louisa did not look disturbed. In fact, if anything, her face assumed a rather smug expression. 'That may not be as difficult as you may think,' she remarked slyly. 'Naturally, I had to wire Mr. Thorne of Annabel's accident. I sent the cable this morning, and of course I had to tell him that Miss Harding had not yet arrived.'

'You ...' Christopher bit off an epithet. 'Emma, come along. I can't stand any more of this.'

Emma followed him up the stairs. Her mind was in a turmoil. She felt an acute sense of guilt, no matter how Christopher might try to spare her feelings. She only hoped the rest of the staff were not all going to be as antagonistic towards her as Louisa Meredith obviously was.

Christopher led the way along a wide, pile-carpeted corridor to Annabel's bedroom. Opening the door, he looked in, and seeing the child, he said: 'Hello, Annabella!'

The squeal of laughter this aroused caught Emma's heart as she followed him into the room. Annabel Thorne was sitting in the centre of an enormous bed which dominated a room decorated unmistakably for a young girl. Pink roses on the wallpaper were repeated on the satin bedspread, while one corner of the room had been taken over by a playhouse, the open door of which revealed a miniature kitchen and dining-room with a sink and cooker, tables and chairs. Annabel, herself, was small and very dark, like Damon, with long hair and a small elfinish face. She was dressed in blue, brushed-nylon pyjamas, and was looking straight at her father's cousin with undoubted pleasure in her expression.

Maybe, with her father being away so much, she transferred much of her affections to Christopher, thought Emma shrewdly. But she also felt a sense of relief; after Damon's peremptory demands, she had convinced herself his daughter must be a problem child, requiring specialized nursing.

'Chris, Chris,' she was saying now. 'You're back! How marvellous! Have you brought Miss Harding with you?'

'Yes, she's here.' Chris drew Emma forward, indicating she should sit down on the bed. 'She's very nice, too, so don't you misbehave yourself and have her sent away.'

Annabel giggled, and reached for Emma's hand. 'Hello,' she said.

'Hello, Annabel,' said Emma gently. 'And how are you after your dip?'

Annabel's face sobered. 'Wasn't it terribly naughty? Miss Meredith nearly had a fit. Tansy was upset too, but she didn't go mad, and send Daddy a cable and everything. He'll be furious, and I'll get into trouble.'

'With due cause,' exclaimed Chris severely. 'Good heavens, young Annabel, you could have been drowned!'

'I know. I know. Miss Meredith has told me all about it. Anyway, she makes me stay in the house all the time now Brenda's gone. Brenda was nice. She let me go anywhere.'

'Yes, but she was with you,' Chris reminded her. 'Anyway, don't worry about it any more. Miss Harding will be able to take you out now. As for your father; he's in Hong Kong. I doubt whether he'll fly several thousand miles just to chastise you.'

'I hope not,' Annabel sighed.

'Well, chicken, I must go. Got to see Helen, and let her know I'm back. I'll be back to see you later. Look after Miss Harding, won't you.'

After he had gone, Emma wondered who Helen was. He hadn't mentioned her before. Was she his sister, his housekeeper, maybe? She shook her head. Doubtless she would find out in good time. She only hoped Damon Thorne did not decide to return to Sainte Dominique. She had hoped to be settled in here before she had to encounter him again. His presence aroused too many memories, and she was afraid of her own feelings, in spite of the past.

Annabel distracted her by reaching out a questing hand and lifting a huge doll from the end of the bed. 'This is Patricia,' she said, breaking the silence which had fallen since Chris's departure. 'Don't you think she's very pretty?'

Emma bit back the words which sprang to her lips. The doll's hair was half torn out, and matted, its arms and legs scratched and chipped; its face was battered and quite ugly.

'I . . . why . . . of course, Annabel, she's beautiful,' she said, accepting Patricia when Annabel handed her to her. 'What beautiful clothes she's wearing. Is this your favourite dolly?'

Annabel nodded, satisfied. 'Yes, I've had her since I

47

was three. She was with me when ... when ...' She halted, and Emma silently completed the sentence. Poor Patricia. No wonder she looked so distressed. 'Will I be able to get up tomorrow? Miss Meredith said I must stay here today, because of the shock I got yesterday, but I won't have to stay here tomorrow, will I? Not now *you're* here.'

Emma smiled. 'Of course not. Tomorrow morning, you and I will take a walk round the island, and you can tell me all about it.'

'All right.' Annabel sounded pleased. 'I used to know it quite well. Before ... well ... before the accident, we came here often, Daddy and I.'

There was a sound from the doorway, and an elderly woman came into the room. She was leaning heavily on a stick, but her wrinkled features were bright and alert, and she smiled warmly at Emma, who rose abruptly to her feet.

Annabel had an acute sense of presence. 'Is that you, Tansy?' she asked, and the old woman answered:

'Yes, I'm here. I've come to show your new nurse her room. I expect she would like a wash before lunch.'

Emma nodded appreciatively, and Annabel said: 'Can she have lunch here, with me? Can she, Tansy, can she?'

'If she wants to, I don't see why not,' replied the older woman. She turned to Emma fully. 'As you've heard, everyone calls me Tansy. My real name is Hester Tansfield, but you can call me Tansy like the rest. You're Emma Harding, is that right?'

'Yes, how do you do?' Emma glanced back at Annabel. 'I'm awfully sorry I didn't get here yesterday. The accident ... it must have been dreadful.'

'Ay, away with you. We get over these little troubles,

don't we, Annabel love? It was a dreadful thing, but accidents will happen, and only that creature Meredith panicked herself silly. Cabling Mr. Thorne indeed! Sure, he'll think the child was injured in some way. She wasn't in the water above thirty seconds.'

Emma reserved judgment. Tansy was old, and so long as Annabel had suffered no physical harm she did not seem to mind. Emma was more concerned with the mental reaction Annabel might have had. In her state, the sudden submersion in water, the terrifying paralysis the fall must have brought upon her, all added up to quite a frightening experience. She determined that at the first opportunity she would teach Annabel to swim. Then accidents of that type would never happen again.

During lunch Annabel gave Emma a comprehensive description of her life here on Sainte Dominique.

'I usually work with Miss Meredith during the mornings,' she said, 'then I rest after lunch for an hour, and then Brenda, Miss Lawson, you know, she used to take me for walks, and sometimes we had Carlos take us out in the launch. Carlos lives here, his wife is Rosa, she works in the kitchens. I expect you'll get to know them all in time.'

Emma smiled. 'I hope I shall. Tell me, Annabel, honestly now, do you see anything at all? Any shapes, or shades, or colours of any kind?'

Annabel shook her head. 'No, nothing. It's just black, that's all.' She shrugged. 'I've got used to it now. It was awful at first, but now I don't mind so much. Everyone is so kind, and Daddy . . . well . . . he used to worry about me a lot. But that was no good, was it? I mean it wasn't his fault, or anything. So I decided I might as well accept it.'

Her way of talking was very adult. Her accident had

obviously cut her off from relationships with children of her own age, and living constantly with adults had prematurely increased her vocabulary.

'Tell me,' said Emma, helping herself to a fresh peach, 'are there no other children on the island, with whom you could be friendly? I mean, what do you do for playmates?'

Annabel sighed. 'I have none. No one would want to play with me, anyway. I'm blind. I can't run after a ball, or swim or anything.'

Emma felt an overwhelming sense of compassion. 'But, darling,' she exclaimed, unconsciously allying herself with the child's point of view, 'there's no possible reason why you shouldn't swim, and play, like other children. After all, lots of blind people swim and water-ski and do all the things any sighted person can do. There are people in London who go about every day doing exactly as sighted people do. After all, like you, most blind people have very acute senses, and they use them to good effect. It's good that you've accepted your condition, but now don't you think you ought to try to live naturally with it?'

Annabel shrugged, staring at Emma with those vacant blue eyes intensely. 'Do you think I could, Miss Harding? Do you really think I could?'

'Yes, I really think you could,' Emma smiled. 'And that's why I'm here, to help you. We'll soon have you swimming like a fish. It's criminal to live here and not enjoy the water.'

Annabel nodded. 'It sounds marvellous, I know. But you see, Brenda didn't swim, and she couldn't teach me, and Daddy has always said the water was dangerous.'

'Well, we'll have to prove him wrong,' said Emma

firmly, unable to prevent a feeling of compassion for Damon Thorne himself. If he was afraid for his daughter's safety to that extent, it proved he was not as unfeeling as he would have her believe.

Apart from Louisa Meredith's antagonism, Emma's first days at Sainte Dominique's Cay were quite enjoyable. She had the run of the house, which was quite large, and apart from Damon's study which was on the ground floor, she had complete freedom of movement. There seemed an enormous amount of servants, but as they all had their own particular duties, they did not get under each other's feet. Tansy seemed to have taken over the running of the house in Damon Thorne's absence, but Louisa wielded her authority as governess to the full.

Emma discovered that the island was a mere half-mile wide by two miles in length, and its whole coastline was edged with beaches and coves of undoubted beauty. Fringed with palm trees, the beaches were pearly white in places, and in others tinged with the pink of coral, crushed into tiny fragments.

Sainte Catherine, across the water, was clearly visible from the house, and like Sainte Dominique had only the one main building on it; Christopher Thorne's house.

Further along the beach from where Emma had landed there was a wooden wind-break, and several boats were pulled up on to the shingle, and to the leeward side of the island, a yacht was anchored, out in a small cove, and Emma discovered from Annabel that that was her father's boat.

'He likes sailing,' she said one morning, as they were walking along the beach before breakfast. 'I've been on the yacht, but I have to wear a life-jacket and a safety harness, and it's not very comfortable when it's hot.'

Emma squeezed her hand. 'Well,' she said, 'we must start our swimming lessons, and then maybe you won't have to wear a life-jacket all the time.'

'Oh, yes, please!' Annabel was excited. 'It would be super if I could swim before Daddy comes again. I hope he doesn't come back to be cross with me for falling in the pool. Louisa shouldn't have cabled him.'

'I expect she thought she was doing the right thing,' remarked Emma thoughtfully. 'After all, you could have been hurt.'

'If Chris had been here, he wouldn't have let her do it,' said Annabel.

'No, perhaps not,' Emma agreed. 'But that's not to say he would be right. You love Chris, don't you?'

Annabel smiled. 'Oh, yes. I miss Daddy an awful lot, and Chris tries to make up for it. But Helen doesn't like him coming here often. I think she's jealous of me. Do you think that's silly?'

Emma frowned. 'I don't know. Who is Helen?'

Annabel shrugged. 'She's Chris's wife. Didn't you know?'

Emma was staggered. Not particularly because of her own feelings, but because of the casual way Chris had acted. The fact that he had *kissed* her, for instance. Was that why Louisa despised him so? Had he tried the same tactics on her and met with a rebuff?

Emma swallowed hard, and mentally stiffened her shoulders. If Louisa thought that she, Emma, had known of his married state and still condoned his behaviour it might account for a little of her antagonism. No wonder she had been so annoyed with them for staying overnight in Nassau! And as another thought struck her, Emma flinched. What construction might Damon Thorne put on her actions? Despising her as he so obviously did, was it not probable that he might think the worst? He could hardly be expected to believe that Emma did not know that Chris was married. Did he wear a ring? She couldn't remember seeing one, but she ought to have thought about it, at least maybe even asked him. But that was ludicrous, her brain ridiculed her reasoning. A girl didn't immediately ask a man whether he was married, the minute she met him. But would Damon Thorne realize that, and if not would he consider her actions disgraceful, and hardly fitting for those of the nurse-companion who was taking charge of his only child?

Emma shrugged. What of it? she argued with herself. If he dismissed her and sent her home to England, surely that was what she really wanted. She could easily take up the threads of her life. Johnny would be delighted, she was sure.

And yet she was reluctant now. Whether it was the pull of the islands, whether she basked in the warmer climate, she wasn't sure, but what she was sure of was that since meeting Annabel Thorne her feelings had somehow changed. No one could know Annabel without being supremely conscious of her courage in the face of such disability, and Emma knew that she wanted to stay with her, help her to overcome her difficulties, and one day see her completely restored to health. She wanted to talk to Damon Thorne about her blindness, she wanted to learn the truth of the specialists' reports, and most of all she wanted to give her the love and affection of which she had been deprived on the death of her mother.

CHAPTER FIVE

HONG KONG was hot, very hot, with the kind of damp heat that saps the energies, and jars the nerves. Damon Thorne paced restlessly about the spacious departure lounge of the international airport, disregarding the pleas of the airport officials, who suggested he should retire to the V.I.P. lounge, and partake of some tea, or coffee, or whisky, if he preferred it. But Damon was in no mood to be placated, and more than one of the officials had suffered the knife edge of his sarcasm. Even Paul Rimini, his personal assistant who accompanied him, couldn't persuade him to relax. They had been waiting at the airport for the best part of two hours now, their Boeing having developed a fault at take-off, and no substitute yet available.

His personal assistant approached him again. Paul Rimini, was a tall slim young Italian, with the dark hair of his race, and exceptionally good looks. He accompanied Damon everywhere, and they were good friends. He knew Damon was impatient to leave for personal reasons, and the prolonged delay infuriated him.

'Say, I could use a drink, sir,' he said. 'Couldn't we find a bar.'

Damon rounded on him. He knew the fact that he felt hot and that his clothes felt as though they were clinging to him in this atmosphere, was responsible in part for his ill-humour, but it didn't prevent his irritability.

'Alcohol! Is that all you think about?' he snapped angrily. He unbuttoned his shirt beneath his tie and ran a raking hand through his thick hair. 'Hell, sorry, Paul. I know it's not your fault, but when are we likely to get out of this sweltering place?'

Paul grinned amiably. Fortunately, he knew Damon too well to be concerned about his moods. 'I'll go see if there's any news,' he said. 'Then maybe we'll have a drink, hmm?'

'All right. Go see what these creeps are doing.'

A young Chinese girl was watching him across the width of the lounge. She was seated, legs crossed, on one of the low couches, her cheongsam slit to thigh level. Damon was aware of her scrutiny, and of the fact that she was attracted to him. He had not lived so long without being aware of his charm so far as women were concerned, but his interest in them was only fleeting. There had only been one woman he had really wanted to marry, and that was Emma Harding. Although that was in the past now, it still infuriated him when he recalled her refusal.

He shrugged these thoughts away, concentrating his attention on the tip of his cigar between his fingers. It was no use remembering his association with Emma in that way. She was now again, just another of his employees, and it ought to please him that she had at last been subjugated to his wishes. But it didn't somehow. He despised himself for blackmailing her as he had done, even if she deserved his contempt.

The Chinese girl had risen to her feet and walked towards him, stopping in front of him. She held an unlighted cigarette in her fingers.

'Please,' she said, indicating the cigarette, and Damon shrugged, and feeling in his pocket, produced his gold lighter. He allowed her dark eyes to hold his as she lit the cigarette, cupping his hand momentarily, and then smiling her thanks. 'I am afraid I have mislaid my lighter,' she exclaimed, her voice light and tinged with an accent.

'My pleasure,' returned Damon smoothly, and glanced round impatiently for Paul. Where had he got to?

'You are flying to San Francisco?' she asked conversationally.

'Eventually,' agreed Damon heavily.

'So am I.' She smiled wider. 'Maybe you would let me buy you a drink to show my appreciation.' She laughed softly. 'For the light, of course.'

Damon's eyes narrowed. 'I don't think that's a very good idea,' he said coolly. 'My assistant and I are going to the bar.'

She would not be snubbed. 'So am I,' she said easily.

Damon drew on his cigar. He could quite simply be rude to her and get rid of her that way, but it was not in his nature to offend people indiscriminately. He saw Paul returning, and gave him a derisively mocking glance over the girl's head. Paul half-smiled, and joined them. He was used to his employer's magnetism attracting all kinds of females.

'My assistant,' remarked Damon, omitting purposely to ask the girl's name. 'Paul, have you any news?'

'Yes, some. They reckon another fifteen minutes, and the plane will be ready for take-off. It was only a minor fault, after all.'

'It's taken them long enough to discover that,' muttered Damon, with some sarcasm. 'However, I guess we do have time for that drink now. Will you excuse us?' He bowed his head politely towards the Chinese girl, and saw that at last she seemed to have realized he did not welcome her company.

He walked across the lounge with Paul, who glanced back pointedly and said: 'Obviously, she didn't want you to be bored any longer.'

Damon grinned. 'Obviously. Unfortunately, I'm not in the mood for seductive oriental females.'

The cable caught up with them in Los Angeles. They were staying at the Royal Bay Hotel while Damon visited the Thorne Chemical Plant out at Thorneville, the township which had grown up around the enormous scientific laboratory. It arrived on their second evening, when they were sitting at the bar, having pre-dinner aperitifs.

Damon opened it casually, expecting to find some new information about one of his companies. It was a complete surprise to him to find Louisa Meredith's name at its foot. He read her remarks carefully, then tossed the cable to Paul, who had been studying Damon's reactions curiously. Paul read the cable and grimaced.

'Serious, do you suppose?' he asked.

Damon swallowed his drink, and ordered another Scotch. Then he read the cable again, more slowly. Louisa's comments were sharp and to the point. Annabel had fallen into the pool, had almost drowned, in fact, and his new nurse-companion had not as yet arrived.

He accepted a cigarette from Paul, then shrugged his broad shoulders. 'I guess it's possible Louisa's histrionics are over-played,' he remarked. 'Nevertheless, Annabel did fall into the pool, and could have been seriously hurt.' He drew on his cigarette deeply, and folded the cable again.

Inside, he felt coldly angry. Why hadn't Emma Harding arrived? The cable was dated the day after she had been expected. Where the hell was she? He was angry, too, to know that her absence disturbed him intensely, quite apart from Annabel's accident. She was the only woman who had ever had this effect on him, and because of it he felt he could willingly crush her. His life had taught him many things; the power of money; the power of his own attraction; the power of intelligence above all things. Before the mighty Thorne Chemical Corporation developed into the combine it was today, Damon himself had been just a research chemist, with an honours degree in physics. He had known all types of women, from ordinary typists who worked for him, to highly specialized and intelligent women in his own field, but only one had ever held any power over him. Always he had held the upper hand, always he had called the tune. It was soul-destroying to know that the only woman he had ever loved did not give a thought for his feelings.

Paul broke into his reverie. 'What are you going to do?'

Damon glanced at him. 'What do you mean?'

Paul half-smiled. 'I can guess what's going through your head. You're the child's father, after all. And where is this nurse you employed?'

Damon stubbed out the cigarette. 'That is the question. Still, I guess she'll be there by now. It's possible she was delayed.' He was cooling his temper.

Paul laughed. 'Did you say Chris was meeting her? I wouldn't put it past our fair gallant to delay her in Nassau. After all, he doesn't have much of a life with that jealous wife of his.'

Damon swallowed his Scotch. 'I hope you're wrong,'

he said harshly. 'Whatever Helen is like, Chris is married, and that's that.'

Paul stared at him. 'So what! You didn't give a damn when he made the running with Louisa last year, and the year before that, come to think of it.'

'Mind your own blasted business,' muttered Damon savagely. 'Get me another drink, and then ring the airport. We're catching the next available flight to Florida. I guess we can pick up the Beagle there, can't we?'

Paul looked astonished. 'I guess we could. If I make the necessary arrangements.'

'Good. Then do it.' Damon lit another cigarette. Paul finished his drink, shrugged, and walked through to make the phone call. Something had upset Damon, something he said, but what? Surely this Emma Harding, whatever her name was, meant nothing to him. In the six years he had been with Damon, he had never known him take more than a transitory interest in any woman, and there had been plenty, since Elizabeth was killed. Not that theirs had ever been a happy marriage, and only the child had prevented a break-up within a few months of the actual wedding. Elizabeth was beautiful, yes, but cold and hard, and Paul had never been able to figure out why Damon married her.

Damon was alone when the slim figure of a woman slid into the seat beside him. She allowed her fingers to trail along the sleeve of his jacket, and Damon, absorbed in his thoughts, gave an involuntary start.

'Hello,' she said. 'Remember me?'

Damon sighed. Dressed tonight in a cheongsam of royal blue figured silk, she was very attractive, her straight hair long and smooth down her back. He half-turned towards her, diverted from the abyss of his thoughts. She smiled, her lips very red, her eyes heavily made up. The triple string of pearls around her throat could be real, he thought. If they were, she wasn't interested in him for his money.

'I remember,' he replied lazily. 'Can I buy you a drink?'

She nodded. 'A cocktail, but please, I'll pay.'

'When I'm with a lady, I pay,' remarked Damon abruptly, beckoning the bartender. He ordered her a cocktail and a whisky for himself. 'Who am I buying a drink for?'

She seemed to hesitate for a moment, and then: 'Tsai Pen Lung.'

He glanced at the rings on her fingers. 'Madame Tsai Pen Lung?'

She agreed. 'And you?'

'Thorne. Damon Thorne,' he replied, offering her a cigarette.

'What are you doing in San Francisco, Mr. Thorne?'

Damon shrugged. 'Business,' he replied vaguely.

'You own the chemical plant out at Thorneville,' she said slowly.

Damon frowned. 'Not exactly, I own a piece of it.' He wondered how she had found that out. If she had not known his name, why had she immediately associated him with the plant? Thorne was not an uncommon name.

She was looking round the bar, studying the other customers. Her eyes were shrewd, and this close he could distinguish tiny lines about her eyes which despite her youthful figure belied her age.

'Why are you in San Francisco?' he asked, attracting her attention.

She shrugged. 'I live here,' she replied smoothly, and

60

that was all. Damon felt piqued. She seemed interested in his movements but had obviously no intention of divulging her own affairs. She must be aware that he wanted to ask what she had been doing in Hong Kong, but she volunteered no information, nor did she encourage him to ask.

She looked at him smilingly. 'You are leaving San Francisco soon?'

Damon hunched his shoulders. This direct questioning was annoying him. 'Maybe,' he said coolly. 'Maybe not.'

'But you are an American,' she said firmly. 'Your accent is unmistakable.'

'I was born in the States,' he agreed. 'Were you?'

'No,' That was all. Again the brick wall, he thought irritably, looking round to see whether Paul was returning yet. If she didn't want to talk, why had she approached him in the first place? Then, as though relenting, she went on: 'I was born in Peking. My family still live there.'

'I see.' Damon nodded. 'Tough.'

She shrugged. 'For some. Don't you believe in the Communist state, Mr. Thorne?' She laughed. 'Of course, you wouldn't.'

'Why, of course? Because I am a capitalist, I suppose. And yet I can see the advantages of equality. My one concern is that there can never be complete equality, and so, as in George Orwell's book, when one government lapses, another takes over. Better the devil you know, is my opinion.'

She chuckled. 'Are you a fatalist, Mr. Thorne?'

'Maybe.' He grinned. 'This is a strange conversation for us to be having.' He looked round, a little restlessly, and rose to his feet as he saw Paul returning. Paul raised his eyebrows when he saw who Damon's companion was, but Damon did not introduce them. Instead, he excused himself, and drew Paul half out of the bar before asking him what he had achieved.

Paul sighed. 'We leave in approximately forty minutes for the airport,' he said, grimacing. 'There were two cancellations on the flight, so I took them. Did I do right?'

Damon nodded, and Paul smiled. 'What about Lotus Blossom?'

Damon grinned. 'Tsai Pen Lung,' he murmured mockingly. 'I don't know. I guess she just recognized a familiar face.'

Paul looked sceptical. 'It's more likely she's been combing every expensive bar in 'Frisco to find you,' he remarked. 'It was obvious you would be staying somewhere like this.'

Damon shrugged. 'So what? There's no law against it.'

'Are you interested?'

Damon tightened the knot of his tie. 'What do you think?'

'I don't know. She's very attractive.'

Damon walked towards the exit, followed by Paul. 'Yes,' he said lazily. 'Her, and a million like her.'

CHAPTER SIX

EMMA took her hand gently away from Annabel's middle and said:

'Go on, keep going, you're doing marvellously!'

Annabel's tanned little arms moved rhythmically, and her legs followed the pattern. She was swimming, actually swimming, for the first time in her life. And it was wonderful!

Then she felt Emma's hands round her waist, dipping her legs down until she was standing again, her feet on the tiled floor of the pool.

'Was I swimming?' she gasped excitedly. 'Was I honestly?'

Emma laughed. 'You were, darling, and all on your own. You did twelve strokes completely alone.'

Annabel hugged herself. 'Oh, Emma,' she gasped, 'won't Daddy be surprised when he comes? I mean, he wouldn't even let me go in the pool at all. He said it was too deep. I had to paddle at the water's edge, and only if he was with me.'

Emma helped her out to sit on the side, their feet dangling in the water. Emma was wearing a white two-piece bathing costume, and already her skin had acquired a light tan. With her dark hair it was very attractive, and she knew the climate agreed with her. She had written twice to Johnny, but had received no reply as yet, but that didn't really surprise her. He was a terrible correspondent. She had settled down very well, and even Louisa Meredith seemed less of a dragon than she had done at first.

Perhaps that was due in part to Emma's annoyance with Chris. He had come over on her third morning, and, as casually as could be, had announced that he was taking Emma and Annabel out for the day. He had skin-diving equipment, and a huge picnic basket in the launch, which he was steering himself today, and he obviously saw nothing for Emma to object about.

But Emma had been angry with him. She asked him why he had not bothered to tell her he was married, and he had shrugged and said:

'Helen and I don't have a normal marriage. She can't have any kids, you see.'

Emma was horrified at this cold dismissal of his wife. 'But surely you could adopt a child, if that's all that's wrong,' she exclaimed.

Chris had shrugged again. 'I don't want anybody else's kids. I want my own,' he replied. Then catching her hand, he said: 'You're much too attractive for me to be able to leave you alone. Don't play hard to get too long. I may get impatient.'

Emma was outraged. She told him in vituperative tones that she despised him for his attitude towards his wife, and that she wouldn't dream of going out with him.

Annabel, who had barely understood half of it, was disappointed, but Emma made it up to her by spending more time than usual with her in the pool, and gaining the child's complete confidence.

Chris had gone away in a rare ill-humour, and Emma hoped he would not find excuses for reporting her behaviour to Damon. It was unlikely, she was sure, for he could hardly say anything to Damon without incriminating himself, and somehow she didn't think he would do that. That night she had felt a little remorseful that their brief friendship should be so roundly shattered, but she also knew that simple friendship was not all Chris wanted.

And so Louisa had softened a little, and they now observed a kind of armed truce, and Emma thought they might, conceivably, eventually become friends. Apart from Louisa, and Tansy of course, there was no one else to talk to, and Annabel's conversation, although adult in some ways, could not take the place of the friendships she had made in the hospital in England.

The sun was hot on their shoulders as they sat on the side of the pool. It was late afternoon; Annabel had had her rest, and then she and Emma had sought the refreshing coolness of the pool. Annabel's bathing costume had been a yellow one-piece affair which had revealed little of her young body, so Emma had obtained some pieces of towelling from Tansy, left over from a pair of bathroom curtains, and made Annabel a bikini which suited her much better. Already she was much browner, and the exercise in the water was strengthening the muscles of her legs.

Annabel lay back lazily, turning her face up to the sun. 'Do you think I'll be able to see again one day?', she asked unexpectedly.

Emma hesitated. She didn't want to raise false hopes in the child's mind, but on the other hand she was aware that Annabel's blindness could be due to a mental block, as much as a physical defect. Whenever she tried to talk to the child about her mother, she came up against a brick wall, as though Annabel was hiding something, and was afraid to say anything for fear of exposing her secret. It was this, combined with a positive lack of facial scars, which led Emma to wonder whether it might be possibly a psychological form of blindness. It was possible, but so little was known about these kind of blockages that one could never be certain.

The sound of a helicopter overhead startled them both, and Annabel sat up excitedly. 'Emma, Emma,' she squealed excitedly. 'It's Daddy, I know it is!'

Emma's nerves jangled unreasonably. Could it actually be Damon Thorne? Had he come back sooner than expected because of Annabel's accident? And what interpretation would be put on the night she had spent in Nassau with Chris? For inevitably this would be brought out into the open.

'Does your father usually arrive in a helicopter?' she asked, as the noise of the craft, and the whirring blades, came irrevocably closer.

Annabel smiled. 'Sometimes,' she said, grasping Emma's hand. 'Could we go to meet him?'

Emma looked down at their scanty attire. There was no time now to go and change, and they could hardly go to meet Damon Thorne, dressed like water-nymphs. 'I think we'll wait here,' she said gently. 'After all, he'll be surprised to find you in the pool.'

Annabel nodded eagerly. 'Of course. I forgot. Do you think he'll like my new bathing suit?'

'Oh, I'm sure he will,' said Emma, leaning back and lifting a red and white striped towelling jacket from off one of the loungers by the pool. She slid her arms into the wide sleeves and drew it over her shoulders, wrapping it closely about her. She had no desire for Damon Thorne to think she was flaunting herself in front of him.

The noise abated, and then there was silence, until the sound of footsteps heralded Annabel's father's arrival. For it could be no one else.

The pool was at the rear of the building, but the

helicopter had landed in a clearing just along the beach from the house, and Damon and another man came walking through the belt of palms, up towards the house. Damon was dressed in a dark blue lounge suit, and carried a briefcase in his hand. The other man, who was younger, wore a light grey suit, and carried a light suitcase. Damon, to Emma, seemed bigger than ever, and her heart seemed to leap into her throat, making her breathless.

Annabel sprang up, holding Emma's hand, and said: 'Let's meet him, Emma, *please!*'

Emma directed her towards her father, and Annabel, startlingly sure-footed, sped across the grass and coral sand to where her father was emerging through the trees.

Damon caught his daughter in his strong arms, and lifted her easily into the air. 'Hello, Annabella,' he said, using the same name for her as Chris had done. 'You're looking very pretty today.'

'Am I, am I, Daddy?' Annabel's voice was high and excited. 'Paul, Paul, it is you, isn't it? Do you think I'm pretty?'

'Gorgeous!' agreed the other man, laughing. 'A bikini, no less. Where did you get that?'

'Emma made it for me,' said Annabel, settling herself on her father's shoulder where he had seated her. 'And guess what? I can swim!'

Emma watched Damon's face register this. His eyes turned to Emma for the first time, and she was intensely conscious of her bare legs and face, and the damp tendrils of hair clinging to her cheeks.

'Is this so?' he asked sharply. 'Annabel can swim?'

'Almost,' said Emma defensively. 'I didn't see why she shouldn't learn. After all, it will prevent any more dangerous accidents from occurring.'

Damon glanced at Paul. He was staring at Emma with frankly admiring eyes, and Emma couldn't help but smile at his expression. Damon saw that smile, and felt infuriated suddenly. He ought never to have brought her here; it was too much! He had acted like a fool!

Annabel wriggled to the ground and caught her father's hand.

'Will you swim with me?' she asked impatiently. 'Will you see what I can do?'

Damon wrenched his eyes from Emma. 'Of course, honey,' he said softly. 'But Daddy has been travelling for some time. I need a nice cool bath, and a couple of hours' rest just now, but tomorrow ... tomorrow you can miss lessons and spend the whole day with me, hmmn?'

Annabel nodded. 'Oh, yes. And Emma, too?'

Damon did not look up. 'Miss Harding may have other things to do,' he said slowly. Then he did look up. 'But I want to talk to Miss Harding tonight, if she has no objection.'

Emma shrugged, aware that Paul was waiting to speak to her. 'None whatsoever,' she replied, and turned away. 'If you'll excuse us, it's time for Annabel's tea. Will you come and see her before bed?' This was addressed to Damon.

Damon nodded. 'Of course. I'll have a drink and a shower in the meantime.' He looked at Paul. 'Paul, I'd like you to meet Miss Emma Harding, Annabel's new nurse-companion.'

Paul smiled warmly at her, and Emma managed to smile back. 'She's an improvement on Brenda Lawson,' he remarked to Damon, as Emma and Annabel disappeared into the house.

Damon lit a cigarette moodily. 'Yes,' he said thoughtfully. Then: 'Don't get involved, will you?'

Paul frowned. 'What's with this girl?' he asked curiously, but Damon ignored him and walked away into the house.

Emma dressed carefully for her interview with Damon Thorne. Usually, in the evenings, she, Louisa and Tansy ate dinner together in one of the smaller rooms on the ground floor which opened out on to a terrace overlooking the beach at the back of the house, and they did not dress formally for the meal. Often, Emma had worn slacks and a sweater, and she had enjoyed the quiet relaxation of it all.

But tonight there was to be no relaxation. She had been informed by the maid, Ruby, that she and Louisa were expected to dine in the main salon with Mr. Thorne and Mr. Rimini. But that would be after her proposed conversation with Damon. And that was what was uppermost in her mind at the moment.

Eventually, she donned a dark blue hostess gown cut severely, with a high round neckline, wide three-quarter-length sleeves, and dozens of tiny pleats flaring from her hips. It was not really an evening dress, or even a cocktail dress, for that matter, but it seemed suitable attire for a nurse-companion. Her hair she left loose in its usual curving sweep, its darkness showing tiny chestnut lights in the depths. Had she but known it the simplicity of the style of her dress, combined with heavy, almost straight, hair, accentuated the vivid colour in her cheeks, making her look much younger than her twenty-five years.

She had bathed Annabel beforehand, attended to her tea, and then seen her tucked up in bed to wait for the promised visit from her father, so when she was ready she descended the stairs feeling wholly apprehensive.

When she walked into the wide lounge, which was seldom used in Damon Thorne's absence, she found Paul Rimini lounging in an armchair, studying one of Annabel's schoolbooks which had been left on a side table. He sprang up at her entrance and said:

'Hello again. I'm afraid Mr. Thorne isn't down yet. Would you like a drink? A cigarette?'

Emma smiled and accepted a cigarette, but she refused a drink, despite the fact that he poured himself a generous measure of Scotch. Then she walked restlessly over to the open french windows, and stood looking out over the formal gardens at the front of the house. The lounge ran the full width of the house, and the windows at the opposite end opened on to the terrace at the back.

Paul took his drink and joined her. 'Have you settled down?' he asked casually. 'I expect you find the climate agreeable.'

Emma nodded. 'Oh, I do. It's certainly a wonderful place.' She turned to look at him. 'Have you worked for Mr. Thorne long? Annabel tells me you're her father's closest personal assistant.'

'That's right.' Paul shrugged. 'I've worked for Damon for about six years now.' He grinned. 'It's a great job; we travel all over the world. And Damon's a great man to work for. You don't know him very well yet, but believe me . . .'

'Please.' Emma broke in. 'Don't let's discuss Mr. Thorne.' She hesitated. 'You must have known Mrs. Thorne, then.'

'Yes, I did.' Paul frowned. 'She was killed almost two years ago.'

'How tragic!' Emma shook her head, and Paul swallowed half his drink at a gulp. He seemed unsympathetic, and Emma was curious. What had Elizabeth Thorne really been like? Surely Damon must have loved her very much to marry her, and Annabel had been born within a year of their marriage. She felt a tightening of her stomach muscles, and changed the subject.

'Do you spend much time here on the island?' she asked.

Paul lifted his shoulders in a careless gesture. 'Sometimes we come and spend a few months, at others only a few weeks. Sometimes Damon comes alone for a holiday, and I return to my home in Milano.'

'You speak very good English,' said Emma, smiling again, as the tension relaxed.

Paul grinned. 'My mother was brought up in England, although she was Italian, and when she was old enough she went back to Italy and married one of her own countrymen, but she taught me to speak English from a very early age. She is of the opinon that English will eventually become the most universally spoken language.'

I think she was right,' replied Emma, glancing at her watch. It was a little after seven-thirty. Dinner was usually served at eight.

Paul raised his dark eyebrows. '*Che,* I am boring you!'

'No, you're not.' Emma was contrite. 'I just wondered when Mr. Thorne will arrive.'

'He's here,' remarked a laconic voice, and they turned to find Damon leaning negligently against the lounge door. He straightened, and said: 'Will you come along to my study, Miss Harding?'

71

Emma trembled a little as she stubbed out her cigarette and followed him along the corridor to the study which as yet she had not entered. He allowed her to precede him into the room, and then closed the door behind them.

Emma forced herself to concentrate on the decor. It was a comfortable room, the walls lined with bookshelves filled with every kind of literature imaginable. There was a desk under a wide window, with a swing black leather chair, and several comfortable armchairs set around. There was a filing cabinet, and a tape-recorder, and a huge electric typewriter on a smaller desk pushed against the wall. The polished floor was strewn with rugs, and the heavy curtains at the windows were a deep orange in colour.

Damon crossed to his desk, and indicated that Emma should sit down on one of the armchairs. She shook her head.

'I'll stand, if you don't mind,' she said, folding her hands together. 'And will you tell me what you want to say at once, because I hate this suspense.'

He looked sardonic. 'How unfortunate,' he remarked, and helped himself to a cigar before continuing. Then he leaned back against his desk, with his arms folded, and said: 'Why didn't you arrive here on the day you were expected?'

Emma swallowed hard. 'Your cousin met me in Nassau, as you know. He suggested it might be a good idea to stay overnight and see something of New Providence.' She sighed. Put like that it sounded dreadful. She should have insisted that Chris brought her straight to Sainte Dominique's Cay.

'You weren't being paid to stay in Nassau to see the tourist attractions,' he snapped angrily.

Emma compressed her lips. 'Oh, what's the use? You'll never understand, will you? When I arrived Chris had already booked the rooms at the hotel. He seemed to take it for granted we were staying overnight.' She sighed. 'I know I should have insisted, but . . . oh, it's impossible to explain just how it was.'

Damon stared at her piercingly. 'Didn't the fact that he was married mean anything to you?'

Emma gasped. 'I didn't know he was married. You didn't tell me, and he certainly didn't. How was I supposed to guess that? He didn't act as though he was married!'

'I can believe that!' Damon straightened up. 'And what about Annabel? I gather she likes you very much. It's unfortunate you may not be staying.'

Emma stared at him now, completely stunned. He couldn't be serious. He wasn't going to dismiss her just because she had not arrived on the exact day he had stipulated. She was quite prepared to lose a day's salary if he was concerned about the ethics of the affair.

'What am I supposed to glean from that remark?' she asked incredulously. 'That you're going to fire me? That I'm to be sent back to England, and Johnny's discrepancy discarded?'

She deliberately brought up her brother's involvement in all this. After all, it was for this reason he had sought to humiliate her.

Damon shrugged his broad shoulders, and Emma felt very small beside him. His hands could practically span her waist, and he seemed, despite his antagonism, wonderfully dependable. And yet she knew he spared little thought for anyone, or anything, and went ruthlessly after that which he desired.

'With any other employee, without the entanglement

of your brother in this affair, that is exactly what I would do,' he said coldly. 'Unfortunately, in your position you're inviolable, unless I were to incriminate your brother again.'

'You *wouldn't!*' Emma's eyes were wide and anxious.

Damon frowned. 'No, I wouldn't,' he agreed heavily. 'So we'll forget this incident with Chris.'

'And I'm to stay?'

Damon studied her animated expression. His sane, logical brain warned him that he ought to get rid of her now, while he still could do so, but for once he did not react to its bidding.

'I suppose so,' he said, nodding, and Emma smiled.

He frowned again. 'It seems,' he said, 'that our positions are now reversed. I was under the impression that you wanted to stay in England; that your work was there; your promotion to Ward Sister, for example.'

Emma flushed scarlet. 'That was before I met Annabel,' she replied defensively. 'She's an adorable child!'

'Is she?' He looked thoughtful. 'Despite the fact that she's *my* daughter?'

Emma looked at him. 'Why should you imagine that that makes any difference?'

Damon stubbed out his cigar savagely. 'It should, shouldn't it? I mean, that's what all this is about, isn't it?' He swung round to face her. 'There were times when I could have killed you for what you did to me!'

Emma clenched her hands tightly. This was deep water now, and she was losing her composure. Why had he had to introduce a personal note?

'It was for the best,' she said, through clenched teeth. She walked resolutely towards the door, but his voice

74

halted her.

'You've never married; have you never had any regrets?' His voice was husky now.

She turned round. 'Regrets about marrying?'

He reached her in a stride. 'You know damn well what I mean.' His eyes ran appraisingly down the length of her body almost insolently.

Emma shivered nervously. Damon this close was overpowering. She had only to move slightly to feel his body against hers and she felt a kind of agonized awareness that he was waiting for her to do just that. In that paralysing moment she remembered minutely every little thing about him; the hard strength of his body, the mat of dark hairs on his chest, the caressing touch of his hands, and the passionate violence of his mouth on hers when he could no longer control his emotions. All this she had given up, but for his sake, although he was unaware of it. Even at this moment, she could hear plainly Lady Masterham's voice as she said:

'Oh, but Emma, I do think Damon is being terribly courageous, don't you? I mean, a man of his age and affluence, and a pretty little creature like yourself with no money at all! I mean, my dear, people are bound to talk, they're just bound to. And I wonder whether it might make rather an unpleasant impact on the corporation when his competitors learn the weakness he has for you. After all, it's completely out of character, isn't it?' And her eyes added: One can't possibly see what he finds interesting in a nobody like you. But even Lady Masterham had not dared to voice so open a disparagement. But the seeds had been laid, insidiously, and Emma had had to listen to many such comments, each one more pointed than the last, until she was convinced she was doing nothing short of ruining his career, and his life.

She looked up at him now, and shook her head, unable to speak. Damon stared down at her intensely for a moment, and then, when she felt her legs would give out under her, he turned away, and muttered: 'Get out!' in a taut, angry voice.

Emma complied, closing the door softly behind her, and closing her eyes for a moment as she relived those seconds of precarious emotionalism. Then, with a stiffening of her shoulders, she walked back along the corridor to the lounge.

CHAPTER SEVEN

THE next morning, after Emma had breakfasted in her room, she came downstairs to find that her employer and her charge had already gone out together. Louisa gave her the news.

'They've gone out on the yacht,' she said laconically, lighting a cigarette, 'so you and I are superfluous today. Mr. Thorne particularly stated that they wouldn't be back before this evening. I think he's taken her to Aldoro.'

Aldoro was a nearby larger island where most of the produce used on Sainte Dominique's Cay was bought. A daily launch took one of the boys to the market there, and the mail, too, was collected from the Post Office. In addition to this, Aldoro had some superb beaches, with facilities for surfing and water-skiing. It had been where Chris had wanted to take them several days ago.

Emma shrugged now, and wondered what she should do for the rest of the day. She had books to read, which she had brought with her, but she didn't feel like reading, and she had not as yet been able to go to Aldoro market herself and buy some material to make herself a couple of summer dresses. She had bought some clothes in London, but everything was so expensive, and besides, she enjoyed making her own clothes.

Louisa looked up at her, and smiled derisively. 'There's the launch, which Joseph can handle, if you should fancy a trip to Nassau,' she said. Then she rose to her feet. 'Actually, in all seriousness, I wouldn't mind a trip there myself, and as we have nothing else to do

. . .' Her voice trailed away.

Emma's ready smile showed her even white teeth. 'It sounds quite interesting,' she agreed. 'And I was wishing I had some material to make myself some dresses. But what about Mr. Rimini? Won't he expect us to be around?'

'If you're concerned about him, don't be.' Louisa smiled naturally now. 'Mr. Thorne dropped him off at Sainte Catherine's Cay before he left. Paul's gone to spend a day with Chris and Helen. He and Chris have known one another for years. They were at university together.'

'Oh!' Emma felt relieved. 'Then I guess we might indulge ourselves, don't you?'

It turned out to be a very enjoyable day. They had lunch in one of the smaller restaurants overlooking the harbour in Nassau, and then walked lazily along Bay Street, admiring the shop windows. In the busy market place, Emma bought three lengths of material in vivid shades of cotton, and Louisa treated herself to some new pants and an evening overblouse. Afterwards they hired bicycles and visited some of the ruined forts dotted around the coastline, and finished up at the Ardastra Gardens. Louisa knew the town quite well, having lived on Sainte Dominique's Cay for the last two years, and she was less of a demanding companion than Chris had been.

Joseph took them back to the Cay after an alfresco meal of shellfish and salad in the open air, and they felt rather guilty for absenting themselves for so long. As they neared the lights of the island, they saw the silhouette of the yacht lying out in the cove, and knew their employer had returned.

When the two girls entered the house, carrying their

78

purchases, there was no sign of anybody. It was still a little before eight, so they went to change and freshen up for dinner.

'Don't worry about Annabel,' Louisa whispered as they mounted the stairs. 'Tansy always takes charge if there's no one else.'

Emma felt relieved. She had been quite willing to return to the island earlier, but Louisa had insisted there was no need. Indeed, Emma argued with herself, in the week she had been here, she had had no actual time off, and although her evenings were her own after Annabel was in bed, it was not the same as getting completely away as they had done today.

She bathed, and changed into a plain dress of turquoise linen, with no sleeves, and a straight skirt. Then she went down to the lounge. Damon was seated at the low bar which occupied one corner, resting on a high stool, swirling the liquid of his drink round and round in his glass. Tonight he was wearing a charcoal grey lounge suit, and looked dark and attractive. He raised his eyebrows as the only indication that he acknowledged her entrance, and she stood uncertainly, unsure of what to do or say.

'Ha . . . have you had a good day?' she asked, at last, finding her voice.

Damon shrugged. 'I guess so. Have you?'

'Yes. Louisa and I went to Nassau. We did some shopping.'

He bowed his head slightly. 'Tansy told me.'

Emma smoothed the skirt of her dress, and Damon nodded to the stool beside him. 'Come on. I'll get you a drink. How about a champagne cocktail? You used to like them.'

He stood up and walked lazily behind the bar, and

uncorked a bottle. Emma walked nervously across, and seated herself on the edge of the stool, and accepted her drink gratefully. It would help to calm her nerves.

A sound behind them heralded Louisa's entrance, and a few minutes afterwards dinner was served.

'Paul is staying over on Sainte Catherine,' said Damon, as they seated themselves at the table. 'He'll be back later.'

Louisa asked about his trip on the yacht, and asked where they had been. Emma wanted to ask how Annabel had enjoyed herself, but her voice refused to obey her commands, and she would not risk talking a lot until she was more in control of herself. After dinner, Damon excused himself and retired to his study, and Louisa grinned at Emma.

'I rather think our presence is wasted, don't you?' she remarked laughingly. 'Let's take a walk. It's a wonderful night.'

Emma agreed. It was a beautiful night, and it was a shame to stay indoors. She collected a wrap and they strolled along the beach in the moonlight. Louisa was in the mood for confidences.

I want to apologize,' she said seriously. 'When you arrived I behaved very badly, but I'll try and explain why . . .'

'Really,' exclaimed Emma in surprise, 'there's no need.'

'I know. But I'll tell you just the same. When I came here, a couple of years ago, to give Annabel elementary lessons, and eventually to teach her Braille, I got involved with Chris Thorne. It was stupid, I know, and I was old enough to know better, but he is very attractive, and I suppose I was getting a bit desperate.' She sighed. 'Anyway, I had a rather violent affair with him. I knew all about Helen, unlike you as I realize now, but I didn't care. I'd met her, you see, and she's cold and rather heartless, and Chris seemed warm, and tender, and in love with me.' She grimaced. 'How foolish I was! Chris only played with me because there was no one else. Brenda certainly wasn't his type, and he's a restless creature, always demanding new experiences, new sensations.

'It didn't last. About nine months later he was tired of me, and seeking new ground to conquer. That's the whole rotten story! I suppose you think what I did to Helen was pretty selfish.'

Emma sighed. 'I'm not in a position to make judgments,' she said softly. 'But I hope we can be friends now.'

'Of course.' Louisa smiled warmly. 'I've realized I like you, Emma.'

After that first day when Damon took Annabel out, life resumed its usual routine. Damon spent most of his time either in his study, or out with Paul on the yacht, or over at Sainte Catherine's Cay. Annabel saw him for a while every evening, before she went to bed, but Emma thought Damon ought to make more of an effort to spend time with his daughter. Although Annabel didn't say much, Emma could tell that she was disappointed that he had not shown more interest in her feat of learning to swim, and had not even swum in the pool with her.

On the fifth evening, Emma felt she must speak to Damon before it was too late. She had no idea how long he intended to stay, and apart from Annabel's needs, she wanted to talk to him herself about Annabel's condition.

After dinner was over, and Damon had retired to his study, she walked along the corridor and tapped on his door. It was a few moments before he called: 'Yes?'

She opened the door and went in, closing it firmly behind her. He was seated at his desk, studying some papers, and looked astounded when he saw who it was. He pushed away the sheaf of papers, and lay back in his chair.

'Well, well,' he said sardonically. 'What can I do for you?'

Emma twisted her fingers together, seeking for words to begin the conversation. 'It's Annabel,' she said at last. 'I think you're neglecting her.'

Damon sat up with a jerk. 'Do you now? And what authority are you on my shortcomings?'

Emma sighed. 'Well, it's true. You've spent one day with her out of the five you've been here. She doesn't say much, but I can see it in her face, she thinks you don't care.'

Damon rose angrily to his feet. 'Miss Harding,' he said, his voice heavy with sarcasm, 'you carry out your duties admiraby. Good night!'

Emma stared at him, her own anger aroused by his attitude. 'Don't you care whether she has any love and affection?' she cried desperately. 'Is the company of your cousin and friends more important than one blind child?'

Her cruel words struck home, and he paled slightly. 'Don't you dare to speak to me like that!' he muttered furiously. 'Annabel doesn't need me, not while she has Louisa Meredith, and Tansy and you, of course.'

'That's ridiculous! She does need you. You're her father!' Emma felt her eyes filling with hot tears, so frustrated did she feel.

Damon strode round the desk, and his fingers gripped the soft flesh of her upper arms, bruising her by their hardness. His eyes were blazing, their black depths flashing fire. He had removed his tie earlier, and the opened neck of his shirt revealed the beginnings of the black hair which grew on his broad chest. Emma felt her traitorous body weakening as he held her there, lashing her with his tongue, telling her that she hadn't the faintest idea of the needs of any human being.

She struggled unsuccessfully to free herself, but he was too strong and merely seemed to derive a sardonic amusement from her efforts. He had stopped talking now, and although his eyes still blazed it was with a different kind of fire. The intensity of his gaze sent a wave of heat over her body, and she stopped struggling and stared at him.

Slowly and deliberately he pulled her towards him, close against the hardness of his body, and his hands encircled her throat menacingly. Then, with a kind of groan, he lifted her face and put his mouth to hers, with violent passion. With a superhuman effort, Emma stopped herself from responding, and she could tell from the increased tenor of his breathing that he was controlling his temper with difficulty. She had expected him to let her go in disgust, but she had reckoned without Damon's persistence, and instead he continued to kiss her, allowing his hands to caress her back tormentingly, arousing her against her will. Emma's lips parted almost involuntarily, and she was lost. As she felt herself drowning in emotion, she was thrust savagely away from him, almost falling as she caught the arm of a chair to save herself.

She gasped, and stared at him, seeing the naked hatred in his eyes. His kisses had shamed and humiliated her, for she had been unable to hide her feelings.

Damon raked his hands through his hair, and his lips twisted mockingly.

'Thank you,' he said, with derision. 'That's given me much satisfaction. Despite all your denials, you're not as immune to me as you would have me believe!'

Emma trembled, and smoothed her hair with a shaky hand. 'You're despicable!' she said, turning away.

'Oh, surely not,' he remarked mockingly. 'Merely human, that's all. Did you really imagine I might retain some respect for you after the way you acted? It amused me to shake that pathetic façade you present to the world.'

Emma clenched her fists. 'May I go?'

'Out of this room, yes. Away from Sainte Dominique, I think not. You have a lot to atone for.'

With a stifled sob, Emma wrenched open the door, and ran out of the study, and up the stairs to her room. She didn't care just then what anyone thought of her. She just wanted to hide, away from his taunts and criticisms, and most of all, away from the touch of his hands.

CHAPTER EIGHT

IT was only six-thirty when Damon rose the next morning. Restless, and unwilling to explore the reasons for this restlessness, he slid lazily out of bed, pulling on a dark blue silk dressing gown, and crossing to his balcony doors. Despite the early hour the sun was already rising steadily to its zenith, and Damon breathed deeply of the pure, clean air. From his balcony he could see the greenish blue waters of the cove where the *Annabella* lay, rocking gently on the waves, her sleek lines and shining paintwork an invitation in themselves.

Damon turned back into the room, and took a cigarette from his case lying on the dressing table. After the cigarette was lit, he walked back to the balcony rail. From the village settlement he could hear the sounds of communal activity as breakfast was prepared, and children began running about noisily. How uncomplicated their lives were, he thought, broodingly, his mind unheedingly reaching back to what Emma had said about Annabel.

He had dismissed her comments the previous evening without much consideration, but now, with the yacht beckoning him to a day's sailing and skin-diving, he wondered half-guiltily whether, in fact, he was neglecting Annabel because of the memories she aroused in him. It was easy to convince himself that the child was quite adequately looked after by her governess and Tansy, and now Emma herself, but might she be secretly longing for his attention?

He swore angrily, and stubbing out his cigarette, he

lifted the telephone on the nearby ottoman. He asked for Christopher's number and waited impatiently for his cousin to answer. The telephone seemed to ring for ages before it was finally lifted and Chris's sleepy voice said: 'Yes? Who is it?'

Damon frowned to himself. 'Me. Damon. What are you doing?'

'What the hell do you think I'm doing at six a.m.?' exclaimed Chris indignantly. 'I'm in bed!'

'It's six-thirty-five,' remarked Damon laconically. 'Anyway, how does a day out on the *Annabella* appeal to you?'

Chris's voice showed interest. 'It sounds great. Today?'

'Why not?' Damon shrugged his broad shoulders. 'Can you be ready in about an hour? I'll arrange food and so on.'

'Sure thing!' Chris was eager. 'Is Paul going?'

'I guess so. See you.' Damon replaced his receiver, and ignored the sensation of selfishness that prodded at him. He was Annabel's father. He'd decide when and how he would entertain her.

He met Paul in the small morning room where they usually breakfasted. Paul was invariably up early, and usually swam before breakfast. He had obviously done so this morning, for his hair was still damp, and clung to his scalp smoothly.

Rosa brought them breakfast, and during the meal Damon outlined his plans for the day. Paul was willing, but he eyed Damon rather curiously and said:

'What happened last night? Emma disappeared after dinner. Did you see her? I was going to invite her to come for a walk with me.'

Damon helped himself to some kidneys and bacon

before replying.

'She came to see me,' he remarked slowly. 'Then I believe she went to bed. Did she know you were waiting for her?'

'Well, no. But she doesn't usually go to bed so early.' He looked concerned. 'Do you think perhaps she's ill?'

Damon grew impatient. 'Of course she's not ill. Now, when you've finished breakfast you can go see Joseph about the oxygen.'

'All right.' Paul shrugged his shoulders, a trifle bewildered. It was the first time he had felt himself unable to penetrate the mask which Damon presented to the world, and he couldn't understand why.

Damon was alone when Annabel appeared. He was just finishing his third cup of coffee when she entered the room, halting instinctively, aware of the presence of another person.

'Daddy?' she said. 'Is that you?'

Damon swung back his chair, and crossing to her side took her hand. 'Yes, it's me, sweetheart. I'm just finishing. Have you had your breakfast?'

'Yes, thank you.' Annabel nodded, gripping his hand tightly. She and Emma usually ate in the small dining-room which was on the same floor as Annabel's bedroom. Emma had lunch there with her, too, and only ate downstairs at dinner time. 'What are you going to do today?'

Damon compressed his lips for a moment. Had Emma put her up to this?

'I'm going sailing with Paul and Chris,' he replied. 'How about you? How is your swimming progressing?'

'I can swim quite well now,' said Annabel quietly.

'But I don't know what we shall do today. We've swum an awful lot, and sometimes we go beachcombing, and sometimes we sunbathe. But I wish you could come and see me swim yourself. Couldn't you, Daddy? I mean, I hardly ever stay with you.'

Damon sighed, and Annabel, acutely sensitive to his moods, turned a bright red. 'I know,' she said. 'You're too busy.'

Damon felt terrible. This was his daughter, after all, and she thought he was too busy to trouble about her. Whether Emma had encouraged her to speak to him, or whether she had just sensed the idea with her acute perceptions was immaterial actually. She wanted his company, and he could not ignore the unconscious appeal of her small features.

He went down on his haunches beside her and held her between his hands. Looking into her sightless eyes, he said huskily:

'Honey-bunch, just what would you like to do today?'

'Go out with you,' replied Annabel guilelessly. She smiled. 'Like we did that first day you came. Could we, Daddy? Could we? And could Emma come, too?'

'Now hold on.' Damon bit his lip. Taking Annabel with them was one thing; taking Emma too was quite another. 'Paul and Chris and I were going out on the yacht, but there's no earthly reason why you shouldn't come too, if that's what you really want. But Emma would feel uncomfortable with three men.'

Annabel pursed her lips thoughtfully. 'Maybe she would. But I'd be there.' She frowned. 'Well, you could invite Helen to come with us. She hasn't met Emma yet.'

Damon grimaced to himself. 'No, I know she hasn't

met Emma. But maybe she wouldn't want to come. Maybe Emma won't want to come.'

'Well, let's ask them. You phone Helen, and I'll ask Emma. We could have a real party. We could go to one of those deserted cays and I could show you how well I swim.'

Damon half wished he hadn't started this. 'Look,' he said. 'You run and ask Emma what she thinks, and I'll wait and see what her answer is.'

'All right.' Annabel turned and was gone almost before he finished speaking. Damon rose to his feet feeling a little relieved. Surely, after last night Emma would refuse.

But when Annabel came hurrying back to the room, her face was beaming with excitement. 'Emma says she'll come, too,' she exploded boisterously. 'She said if that was what I wanted she couldn't refuse.'

Damon gnawed at his lower lip. 'All right,' he said gruffly. 'I'll ring Chris and ask if Helen will come, shall I?'

'If you think it's really necessary,' said Annabel, in a small voice, and Damon remembered belatedly that despite Annabel's appeals that Helen might come too, secretly she didn't much like Chris's wife. Helen tended to treat her like an invalid, and Annabel wanted nobody's pity. But he refused to spend the day in Emma's company, without another woman present, and so he said:

'I think it's necessary, honey-bunch,' and lifted the telephone.

The *Annabella* was a thirty-five-foot ketch, with a small cabin capable of providing all the cooking facilities necessary for light meals, and a foldaway table, between

89

side bunks which could be used as sitting space. On deck there was plenty of room for sunbathing and the rhythmic rise and fall of the waves was very relaxing.

Emma sat with Annabel, dangling their legs over the side of the yacht, watching the incredibly clear blue sky melting easily beneath a strengthening sun. It was a glorious morning, and she knew that there was nothing more delightful than the prospect ahead of them: a day's sailing and swimming and sunbathing. She was wearing knee-length cotton jeans and a sleeveless sweater, her two-piece swimsuit concealed underneath. She was not even certain she would have the confidence to remove her outer garments despite the heat if there was only to be herself and the three men.

Annabel had told her that Paul was going with them, and Chris, too. She had mentioned Chris's wife, Helen, and said that her father was inviting her also but that she doubted whether she would go.

'Helen doesn't much like sailing,' she said, making a face. 'But if she knows we're going she'll probably come, just out of curiosity.'

Emma smiled at Annabel's old-fashioned way of speaking, and wished there were children she could play with. She was too much in the company of adults.

So now they were aboard; Paul and Damon were hauling up the sails, and soon they would be sailing across the channel to Sainte Catherine's Cay.

Emma had not yet met Helen, and she was loath to do so, particularly as it meant meeting Chris again. She had not seen him since the morning she had told him what she thought of him, and she doubted whether the day could be a success with so many undercurrents lying just below the surface.

Unwillingly her eyes turned to Damon. He was

dressed in brief shorts and a thin knitted courtelle jersey, with short sleeves that revealed the muscular brown length of his arms, so thickly covered with dark hairs. His gold watch glinted on his wrist, while he wore a thin gold chain about his neck on which was a tiny medallion of Saint Christopher. She knew about the medallion; she had used to tease him about it in the good days.

Paul Rimini was dressed in like manner, looking slimmer and younger but no more attractive than his employer. Emma could not help but be impressed by the relationship between these two. They were such good friends and it was obvious Paul respected and admired the older man.

Annabel, wearing a rubber ring which was securely fastened to the yacht's rail, slid her fingers into Emma's confidingly.

'It's wonderful, isn't it?' she said, sniffing appreciatively. 'Oh, I wish every day could be like today!'

Emma squeezed her fingers in return, but did not answer. She was wondering just how much of a fiasco it was going to be. It had been obvious from the start, from Damon's attitude, that he had not wanted her to go with them, and had only asked her because Annabel insisted. But Emma refused to disappoint the child, merely because of Damon's ill humour.

The yacht was moving now, slowly and smoothly, as the wind filled her sails, and gave her freedom. Out of the cove, the sea was calm as a millpond, with only gentle waves lifted by the breeze.

Emma felt the breeze ruffle its way through her hair, and was glad she had secured it back from her face with a wide blue band. She slid her sunglasses on to her nose, and rested back on her elbows lazily. It was impossible to remain indifferent to the day and her surroundings, and she smiled in pure enjoyment.

Paul flung his length beside her, grinning into her face cheekily.

'Hi! Did anyone tell you you're quite a dish?'

Emma chuckled. 'No one ever did. And I don't believe you. You're just one of those amorous Italians I am always reading about.'

'No, really!' Paul protested laughingly. 'It won't take us long to reach Sainte Catherine's. I wonder if Helen will be with Chris.'

'She will!' said Annabel gloomily. 'I expect she'll want to see Emma, if nothing else. After all, Emma hasn't been over to the island yet.'

'No, she hasn't, has she?' Paul frowned. 'Why not, Emma?'

Emma shrugged, flushing. 'No reason. I've never been invited.'

Paul looked sceptical. 'I can guess. Chris!'

'Whatever do you mean?'

'Don't tell me you don't know about Chris's affairs. Louisa, for example.' He studied her appraisingly for a moment. 'That was why Damon was so damned mad, wasn't it? You didn't arrive on the day you should, and cousin Chris was meeting you. Put two and two together . . .'

'. . . and make five,' said Emma dryly. 'I'm sorry to disappoint you, but I only met Chris that one time, and we certainly didn't have an affair!'

'No. But he made a pass at you,' said Paul shrewdly. 'I can tell from your expression that I'm right, but you, having a little more sense than Louisa, must have sent him back with his tail between his legs when you found he was married. Right?'

'That's right,' said Annabel, joining in. 'Chris came a couple of days after Emma arrived, and he asked us to go out with him, but Emma wouldn't go, would you, Emma? And she was so *mad*!'

'Oh, Annabel!' exclaimed Emma, feeling embarrassed at being discussed this way.

Paul looked pleased with himself. 'Good,' he said grinning. 'Good!'

Emma became conscious of a fourth presence, and glanced round to find Damon leaning against the hatch, watching them. He had obviously been able to listen to their conversation, and she wondered what he would make of it.

'Come and give me a hand,' he said, his voice cool and disinterested.

Paul sprang up, and winking at Emma followed Damon back along the deck. Emma sighed, and stared out across the water. Paul was a nice boy; nice and uncomplicated. How pleasant it would be, she thought, to fall in love with someone like that. Someone who would be gentle and kind, and respect you, instead of loving a man who hated her for what he thought she had done to him seven years ago, and who only wanted to hurt and humiliate her.

Helen Thorne was the complete antithesis of anything Emma had expected. Emma had thought Chris's wife would be tall and slim and soignée, but she couldn't have been more wrong. Helen Thorne was small, almost as small as Emma herself, but very plump, with fair hair which was cut short and straight to her head, and wearing shorts and a tight sweater, which drew attention to the thickness of her legs, and the roll of flesh round her middle. She wore plimsolls and white socks instead of sandals, and carried a knitting bag.

93

Damon and Paul greeted her casually, but it was apparent that her eyes were seeking the other female member of the adult party. When she saw Emma looking slim and attractive in her jeans and sweater, rope-soled sandals on her bare feet, her eyes narrowed angrily and she gave Chris a killing glance. Perhaps, thought Emma, he had been passing her off to his wife as some middle-aged spinster nurse, in the hope they would never actually meet. It was the kind of thing he would do, she thought.

Introductions were brief, and Annabel was unusually silent. Emma understood why when Helen squatted down beside the child a few minutes later, and said:

'Hello, darling. How are you? Are you feeling a little better today? This fresh air will do you the world of good.'

Annabel sighed. 'I'm perfectly all right, thank you, Helen,' she said. 'And I never felt better.'

'What a brave girl you are,' said Helen unheedingly. 'Coming aboard a boat like this, and you unable to see or swim.'

Emma gritted her teeth. 'Annabel can swim,' she retorted. 'I taught her.'

Helen looked coldly at her. 'Did you, indeed? I understood that you were her nurse, not her playmate.'

Emma retained her composure with difficulty. 'Annabel and I are the best of friends,' she said. 'We enjoy each other's company, and as I enjoy swimming, I felt sure she would, too.'

'Don't you think that's rather a dangerous occupation for a blind child?' Helen was annoyed, and her pale cheeks were flushed.

'I think Emma knows rather more about that than you do, Helen,' said a quiet voice behind them.

Emma's nerves tingled. Damon was actually defending her. She couldn't believe it.

'Oh, Damon,' exclaimed Helen pettishly. 'You're so seldom here anyway, I hardly think you know the child's feelings about anything.'

Damon went down on his haunches beside them, and Emma felt his knee brush against her bare arm. The touch sent shock waves along her veins, and she moved her arm quickly away.

'Maybe not,' he said huskily, 'but if I know little, you know less, so let's not get embroiled in an argument on a day like this. I'm glad you decided to come Helen. The change will do you good.'

The yacht was anchored at lunch time just off a small atoll which seemed to be composed almost entirely of rock, a tall cliff rising steeply into the sky above a deep water cove.

'Minerva's Stone,' remarked Chris, talking to Emma for the first time that morning. 'Curious formation, isn't it? But a splendid place to swim from; a readymade diving board.'

Emma was staring at the island. 'No one actually dives from the top?' she exclaimed.

'Well, people have, but very few, I'll admit, and I'm not one of them,' admitted Chris. He forced her to look at him. 'Am I forgiven?'

Emma half smiled. 'You shouldn't be.'

'But I am,' he grinned.

'Oh, I suppose so.' She looked away. 'Have you been married long?'

'Ten years. I married Helen when I was twenty. She was twenty-five.'

'Oh!' Emma nodded.

'After lunch Paul and Damon are going snorkelling.

Do you want to come?' Chris's eyes were caressing.

Emma shivered. 'I don't know how. Besides, there's Annabel.'

'Annabel rests after lunch. And I'll teach you.'

'I don't know ...' Emma was reluctant. She was tempted to learn to snorkel but she was troubled about going with Chris. Already Helen was watching them again, and Emma was no husband-stealer.

Damon came across to them at that moment. 'There are hampers of food and beer in the cabin. Do you want it up here?'

Emma knew he wasn't talking to her, and bent her head to avoid his eyes. Chris was saying: 'Oh, up here, Damon. I'll get it,' and then they were alone for a moment.

'What was Chris saying to you?' he asked, his voice low and commanding.

'He ... well ... he asked me whether I would go snorkelling with him after lunch, while Annabel rests.' Emma flushed. 'Don't worry. I haven't agreed. I don't suppose you want me along. That's perfectly all right with me.'

Damon stared angrily at her. 'You've a damned nerve,' he swore furiously. 'Don't treat me like some petty schoolboy!' He looked out across the water towards Minerva's Stone. 'Can you snorkel?'

'No.' Emma turned away, but he turned her back, his fingers hard on her arm.

'Do you want to learn?'

Emma sighed. 'What do you think?'

'All right. I'll teach you myself. You can tell that to cousin Chris when he asks you again.'

Emma wasn't hungry at lunch time, her mind too active with the prospect of spending some time with

Damon that afternoon. It was an exciting prospect, and her nerves were as taut as violin strings.

When Annabel was settled in the cabin for her rest, and Helen had announced her intention of staying aboard the yacht, the three men and Emma climbed into the dingy and using the outboard motor sped across the surface of the water to the sandy beach of the island. Once there, the three men stripped off their outer clothes revealing themselves in swimming trunks. Gathering all her courage together, Emma peeled off her jeans and sweater, and ignored the admiring glances Paul and Chris cast in her direction.

Flippers and masks with breathing tubes were hauled from the dinghy, and Paul and Chris put on their tackle at once. Emma watched them wade into the water, and then with a twist they disappeared beneath the sparkling surface of the waves.

'Easy, isn't it?' remarked Damon, half smiling at Emma's surprised reaction. 'There's nothing to it actually, so long as you don't go too deep. Come on, I'll help you on with your things.'

Emma was shivering as she pulled the flippers on to her feet.

'Are you cold?' asked Damon, frowning. 'Don't go in if you're cold.'

Emma looked up at him awkwardly, as she sat on the sand. 'I'm not cold,' she said. 'Just apprehensive, that's all.'

'With me?'

'Who else?'

Damon shook his head, then removed his sandals and pulled a pair of flippers on to his own feet. 'I won't let you drown yourself, if that's what you're afraid of,' he said mockingly.

Emma staggered to her feet, unsteady in the rubber feet. She watched him until he had finished, and felt that disturbing awareness of him increasing. She had never seen him in swimwear before, and she wondered what he would say if he knew how much she wanted to feel his body close to hers. He despised and humiliated her, but because he thought she was almost indifferent to him. She wondered idly why he should feel so angry, when he had married Elizabeth so speedily after their separation.

Damon handed her the mask and the mouth tube, and put on the same equipment for himself.

'Right,' he said, 'are you ready?'

Emma had to smile. 'As I'll ever be,' she remarked dryly, and stepped gingerly into the water.

Afterwards she wondered at her apprehension, it was so easy. It opened up a whole new world for her, a world of waving fronds, and multi-coloured fish-life, of fantastically shaped coral, and delicate shells. The flippers propelled her forward steadily, and she found they helped her to remain under the water once she got used to them. To begin with, it was difficult not to surface every few minutes, but soon she was exploring deeper, and coming upon the dark shapes of Paul and Chris who grinned encouragingly at her, removing their mouthpieces to demonstrate their ability.

After a while, her legs began to tire, and afraid of cramp, she sought the shallower water, and the warm silkiness of the sand. She sank down wearily, lifting off the mask, and pulling the flippers from her feet. Then she lay back and closed her eyes.

She must have drowsed in the warm sun for a while, because when she opened her eyes again it was to find Damon sitting on the sand beside her tinkering with an oxygen cylinder which he had taken from the boat.

Paul and Chris were diving from a plateau of rock some thirty feet above the pool below Minerva's Stone. They had shed their equipment, and it was lying on the sand near her feet.

She sat up abruptly, shading her eyes with her hand, watching Damon. A cigarette between his lips, he was tightening the valve of the cylinder, and seemed unaware that she had woken.

'Did I sleep long?' she asked, self-consciously.

He glanced at her indifferently, she thought. 'Fifteen, maybe twenty minutes, that's all. I guess you were exhausted. It takes some getting used to.' He thrust the cylinder to one side, and removed his cigarette from his lips. 'Would you like a cigarette?'

Emma nodded. 'Please.' To her surprise he lit the cigarette before handing it to her, and she drew on it gratefully. 'What time is it?'

'A little after three. Relax! If Annabel wakes up Helen can take care of her for a while. I guess you haven't had much free time since you arrived.'

'I have every evening,' said Emma.

'Yes, but that's hardly the same, is it? I mean, every employee is entitled to at least one day off every week.'

'All right. Thank you.' Emma drew up her legs, and hugged her knees, staring out towards the yacht unseeingly. It was nice, she thought, relaxing like this without verbally sparring with Damon every sentence she spoke. Damon had pulled on his light jersey again, and looked broad and muscular. She noticed he had not removed his watch for swimming.

He lay back, drawing dark glasses out of his pocket, and sliding them on to his nose. Then he said, surprisingly:

'Tell me something, Emma; exactly why did you break it up?'

Emma was startled by the unexpectedness of the question. She was off guard and vulnerable. 'You know why,' she replied stiffly.

'I know what *you* said,' he corrected her. 'That there was someone else; someone you'd just realized you were in love with.'

Emma felt her whole body was bright red with embarrassment. 'Must we talk about it?' she asked. 'I mean, it's such a long time ago ...' She wished she could see his eyes, read their expression; she was sure he had put on dark glasses deliberately so that she was at a disadvantage.

'Yes, I think so,' he murmured derisively. 'After all, I'm the one who was *jilted*!'

'Oh, stop it!' she exclaimed. 'You were so badly hurt by it all that you married Elizabeth Kingsford ten weeks after we parted!'

At last she had got under his skin, and he wrenched the glasses off his nose and stared at her with cold, angry eyes.

'I want the truth, Emma,' he muttered furiously, 'and by God, I mean to get it!'

'I don't know what you mean,' she cried, putting the palms of her hands over her ears. But that did not cut out the sound of his voice; the icy derision that was worse than any hot temper could have been.

'Yes, you do,' he said. 'There was no other man, was there? Or if there was, where is he? No, Emma, you had second thoughts, didn't you? After all, you were eighteen, I was thirty-seven, more than twice your age! Why couldn't you have admitted that you thought I was too old for you? Old enough to be your father, in fact!'

'No!' The word was wrenched from her and she stared at him with tortured eyes. 'No, no, *no*! That isn't true!'

Damon's eyes showed their disbelief, and she turned away helplessly. He would never believe her!

Paul and Chris came strolling along the beach towards them, and Emma was relieved. At least it prevented any further conversation of this kind.

'Coming for a swim, Emma?' asked Paul, and she sprang up gratefully.

'I'd love to,' she replied, managing a light smile, and let Paul chase her through the shallows before they both plunged into the deep pool and swam across it swiftly.

The water was refreshing to Emma's hot body, and Paul's obvious pleasure in her company almost made up for Damon's anger. Paul showed her where they could climb out of the water, on to a ledge, and up a kind of winding rock stairway to the plateau where he and Chris had been diving from.

'Can you dive from here?' asked Paul doubtfully. 'Don't attempt it if you'd rather not.' He smiled. 'You can wait here for me.'

'Oh, no,' exclaimed Emma. 'I don't want to wait. I have done a lot of diving at home, in swimming baths and so on, so I'm sure I'll be okay.'

'All right.' Paul grinned and squeezed her hand. 'Did you know that Damon used to dive from the top? When he was younger, of course.'

Emma looked up, shaking her head; it seemed a terribly long way. 'Wasn't that dangerous?' she asked.

'Not really. If you're an expert you can do it. The danger comes during the actual dive, maintaining your balance. If you lose that you could break your back . . .

or your neck!'

Emma swallowed hard. Picturing Damon injured fatally, or crippled, was terrifying. She spent almost an hour with Paul, joined later by Chris while from their ledge they saw Damon take the dinghy back to the yacht and return with Annabel in her swimsuit. They played on the beach, and in the shallows, Annabel demonstrating her swimming skill, her squeals of laughter coming clearly to them across the water.

Later they all went back to the *Annabella* and after drinks turned for home.

Helen insinuated herself between Annabel and Emma on the homeward journey, and said:

'How did you come to get this job, Miss Harding? Are you a children's nurse?'

Emma shook her head. 'No. I was a nurse in a hospital in London, but the prospect of several months in the Bahamas was too good to miss.'

Really, thought Emma as she said this, it was very easy to say. What had started as a painful chore had become unreasonably enjoyable, despite her encounters with Damon. She knew she would rather be here, than back in London, with Damon only a heart-stirring memory of the past.

'Then how did Damon come to choose you?' Helen was still curious.

'I ... I ... applied for the post when it was advertised.'

'Was it advertised? That's unusual for Damon. He usually hires an agent to secure his staff for him.'

Emma flushed. 'Well, in this instance he didn't,' she said shortly.

Helen shrugged, and looked at Emma disbelievingly. Her suspicious mind was already creating situations that didn't exist. For an employee who had only known her employer a very short time she acted very familiarly, and Helen was prepared to believe the worst of anyone who was as attractive as Emma.

CHAPTER NINE

FOR the next couple of days Damon devoted the whole of his time to Annabel. Emma felt quite superfluous, for Damon took over the tasks she had been used to doing, and she managed to stay discreetly in the background. Paul took her to Nassau one afternoon, and would have stayed until after dinner, but she insisted on being back in case she was needed. Besides, she had the feeling that Paul wanted to have a closer relationship than friendship with her, but much as she liked him she had no personal interest in him and did not wish to act otherwise.

She had a letter from Johnny which disturbed her a little. He seemed to be finding it difficult caring for himself, and she hoped he was getting enough to eat. London seemed such a long way away from Sainte Dominique's Cay, and her life there in retrospect seemed colourless and wholly concerned with her work.

Then, three days later, Damon departed early one morning in the helicopter with Paul, and Emma learned, through Tansy, that he had returned to the States to complete his business there.

After he had gone, nothing was quite the same. Just his presence in the house had added a kind of vitality to the days, and now he had gone the place seemed empty. Annabel was regretful, but contented, because her father had shown such interest in her during the last couple of days. He had swum with her, played with her, read to her, and generally amused her. Emma found it difficult to take the place of Damon, even though Annabel obviously had grown fond of her.

A week later they were invited to Sainte Catherine's Cay for the afternoon. Annabel grumbled when Emma said they ought to accept as Helen had issued the invitation, but she finally agreed and they went.

Helen's home was not a bit as Emma would have expected. It was far from clean, as though the servants were not observed very thoroughly, and piles of books and magazines littered the living-room. Chris had shut himself away in his study, and the click, click of his typewriter was all that could be heard of him. Helen put herself out to be more friendly towards Emma, but Emma thought she must be a lazy creature to leave the house in such a state. Helen was dressed sloppily in slacks and a sweater, and her hair needed washing. She knitted interminably, and Emma wondered what she was making, but didn't like to ask. Both she and Annabel were relieved when the time came for them to leave, and Emma hoped she would not have to repeat that experience.

The days slid slowly by. She wrote to Johnny regularly, and received casual notes from him from time to time. Worries about him were her only concern; she refused to admit to the continual ache she felt when she thought of Damon.

Damon was restless.

It was exactly three weeks since he had returned to San Francisco, and now all his work was completed and he and Paul were leaving for London the following day. But this was not why he was restless. Despite his intensive concentration on the job in hand he had been unable to get thoughts of Emma Harding out of his mind, and consequently he was short-tempered and irritable, and even Paul was unable to get through to him.

His evenings had been taken up with invitations from various of his colleagues and friends, who all wanted to see him while he was there. He attended the cocktail parties, the lunches, the dinners, but although he was polite and charming when spoken to, when left to himself he was morose and withdrawn, and he knew Paul could not understand why. He was tempted to tell the younger man of his earlier relationship with Emma and thus reveal his reasons for his attitude, but he was not a man to seek the sympathy of anyone, much less in a situation where he felt he had made a fool of himself.

He had admitted to himself that he was still attracted to Emma even though it might only be the physical attraction which had brought them together in the first place before her personality and warmth had enslaved him, making him desire her more than he had ever desired any woman.

He cursed himself angrily as he paced about the soft fitted carpet of his bedroom at the Royal Bay Hotel. Why did his mind persist in trying to find reasons for Emma's defection seven years ago? Why couldn't he accept what she had told him? But there were too many points on which his calculating brain seized again and again. When she had first broken their engagement he had been so hurt and angry that he had hired a private detective to report to him on her movements. There had been no other man, however much she protested that there had, and his feelings had been trampled when he had had to assume the reasons for her withdrawal had been solely concerned with himself; his age, his appearance, his personality.

And now, to his intense disgust, despite her actions in

the past, he found his traitorous senses stirring at the memory of her smooth lithe body lying relaxed in slumber on the sands below Minerva's Stone.

He lit a cigar, drawing on it violently, and started when there was a knock at his door. 'Come!' he called, peremptorily, glad of the respite from his thoughts.

Paul entered, closing the door behind him, grinning amiably. Reaching into his slacks' pocket for his cigarette case, he said:

'You have a visitor!' He lit a cigarette. 'Madame Tsai Pen Lung!'

Damon stared at Paul incredulously. 'You must be joking!'

'Sorry, but I'm not. I was in the bar just now, getting some cigarettes, when she came up to me. She asked whether we were staying in town long, and naturally I told her we were leaving in the morning.'

'Naturally,' remarked Damon laconically. 'So what?'

'So she invited us for a farewell drink.'

Damon grimaced. 'Damn! Is she in the bar now?'

'Yes, and likely to stay that way.'

Damon flung himself down into an armchair. 'Just when I feel like getting good and drunk!'

Paul shrugged. 'You could have it sent up,' he suggested. 'I might join you myself.'

Damon shook his head. 'I don't feel in the mood for solitary parties. I need company; my own depresses me.'

Paul stared at him. 'Honestly, Damon, what's wrong with you? You've been practically unapproachable since we left the island!'

'There's nothing wrong with me that a good binge won't cure,' remarked Damon. 'Come on, Paul. We'll go down. I can think of worse females I've known.'

Paul sighed, unable to pierce the mask that Damon had somehow assumed. Stretching, he left the room for his own where he donned a tie and jacket before rejoining Damon.

The bar downstairs was crowded, but Madame Tsai Pen Lung must have been watching for them, for as they entered she came purposefully across to join them. Tonight she was wearing an oriental-styled trouser suit, covered in red dragons and crescent moons, with a high mandarin collar and close-fitting pants. Her hair was wound on top of her head in a coronet, while heavy jade hoops hung from her ears.

'Ah, Mr. Thorne,' she said, smiling, including Paul in her greeting. 'I am so glad you were able to join me.'

Damon murmured something politely, and then she led the way across to a small table in one corner of the huge, brilliantly-lit saloon. A waiter attended to them, and when their drinks were supplied she lay back studying Damon intently. There was about her tonight an air of nervousness, which Damon had not noticed before. A tautening of her features, and an awareness, almost of anxiety. The dark oriental eyes darted hither and thither as she spoke to them, as though searching for something, or someone.

Damon shrugged, dismissing his deductions as a hangover from his own particular brand of mental anguish, and determinedly swallowed the remainder of his whisky, and ordered another.

'Do you often come to San Francisco, Mr. Thorne?' Tsai Pen Lung asked, sipping her cocktail delicately.

Damon shrugged again. 'It depends. When I have business here sometimes I stay for many weeks, but at others I may only stay overnight.'

'And you commute to London?'

'I usually spend some time in London,' he agreed, his eyes narrowing, wondering why she was so concerned about his movements. He had noticed she divulged very little information about herself.

'What about you?' said Paul, breaking into their conversation. 'Do you intend staying in San Francisco now you're here?'

She shook her head. 'Maybe, maybe not. It depends whether I am permitted to stay.'

'I'm sure no one could refuse to allow such a beautiful woman as yourself permission to remain here,' said Paul gallantly, catching Damon's eyes mockingly.

'Why, thank you, Mr. Rimini. It is very kind of you to say so, but I regret immigration officials are unmoved by appearances.'

'Appearances can be so deceptive,' remarked Damon coolly. 'After all, what possible attributes can be satisfactorily diagnosed as being particularly undesirable? A priest can look like a devil, and a murderer can have the face of an angel!'

'It is the eyes, I think,' replied Tsai Pen Lung thoughtfully. 'One can usually discriminate honesty in a person's eyes.'

Damon drew out his cigarette case. 'And when one is blind, what then?'

She stared at him. 'You are not blind!' Her tone was incredulous.

'No.' Damon opened the case and offered her a cigarette. 'Did I say I was?'

She swallowed, and shook her head, then took a cigarette, smoothing it between her fingers in a distracted way. Again Damon felt disturbed. There was something troubling her; something playing on her mind, something behind this ambiguous conversation.

He shook himself slightly. It must be the amount of alcohol he was consuming, he thought. He was becoming quite fanciful. Yet he was concerned somehow. He wondered whether if he had been alone she would have confided her problem to him. He inwardly chided himself. Hadn't he enough problems of his own, without pondering the problems of a Chinese girl he had met exactly three times?

Realizing she was waiting for a light, he flicked his lighter hastily and in so doing dropped it. It slid from his fingers and fell with a thud on the soft fitted carpet beneath their feet.

'I'm sorry,' he apologized, looking at Tsai Pen Lung, and discovering her face was chalk-white. She seemed to be looking beyond him, but when he turned his head to see what she was staring at there was nothing. He looked back at her, and then at Paul, who appeared to have noticed nothing amiss and was lazily carrying on a conversation about baseball with a man sitting at his other side.

He frowned, remembered his lighter, and was about to retrieve it when Tsai Pen Lung forestalled him. 'Let me,' she said, and slid down to the floor in a lithe, fluid movement.

Damon glanced round again, his heightened senses aware of someone watching him, or Tsai Pen Lung. It was ridiculous, he knew, and yet among that sea of faces, talking so vibrantly, there was someone who had frightened the girl. But why? Who was there in San Francisco that she could be frightened of? She had only been in the country about five weeks. Who could she possibly have made an enemy of in that time?

His desire to get drunk was fast disappearing. He thought that at least she had lifted a little his shroud of depression. She slid back into her seat, but only momentarily before excusing herself, saying:

'I won't be a moment. The ladies' room, you understand . . .'

Damon rose to his feet politely as she left the table, and then subsided again. What the hell, he thought, irritably, he was behaving as though he cared what happened to her. And yet he had respect for any human being, and although she did not move him emotionally he was concerned about her just the same. He thought maybe when she came back from the ladies' room, he would take her for a meal in the restaurant, and maybe then she would tell him what was troubling her.

He lifted his drink, and realized he still held an unlit cigarette between his fingers. Damn, the lighter, he thought. Tsai Pen Lung must have taken it with her. He glanced round moodily, wondering whether he had been completely wrong about her, and her motives. The lighter was valuable; it had been given him on his twenty-first birthday by his parents, and although being gold with a jewelled monogram its sentimental value far exceeded its intrinsic worth. Had she been merely a thief, using a new method of obtaining her loot? And if so, why hadn't she attempted that kind of trick earlier?

'Give me a light, Paul,' he said, and Paul leaned over to oblige.

'Where's Tsai Pen Lung?'

'The ladies' room, I guess,' remarked Damon, unwilling to admit to his doubts.

Paul frowned. 'What's wrong? Where is your lighter, anyway? Has it run out?'

Damon shook his head. 'Later,' he said testily, and swallowed his whisky. 'Let's have a bottle of that stuff, shall we? It doesn't seem particularly potent.'

Paul beckoned the waiter and ordered a bottle, and Damon consulted his watch. It was exactly six minutes since Tsai Pen Lung left for the ladies' room. He would give her five more minutes and then he would take a walk into the lobby to see whether he could see her. He had no illusions. If she had stolen his lighter there was not a chance in a thousand that he would get it back. But even so he had no intention of simply sitting there waiting without knowing one way or the other.

The minutes elapsed, and Paul, who had given up his conversation about baseball, said: 'She's a hell of a long time, isn't she?'

Damon's temper was rising, and he was in no mood for light chatter, so he did not reply, and Paul shrugged, and helped himself to another drink, idly studying the women, speculating on their attributes to himself for his own satisfaction. They were all smart, most of them very smart with elegant hair-do's and sleek gowns. Their companions were well dressed and mostly middle-aged, with midriff bulge supplied by too much alcohol and too little exercise.

When fifteen minutes had elapsed, Damon rose to his feet, and looked down at Paul angrily. 'I'm going for a walk. See you later.'

Paul rose also. 'Now hang on, Damon! What's wrong? I didn't know you cared!'

'I don't. She's got my lighter,' said Damon in a taut, furious tone. 'Get it!'

Paul hunched his shoulders. 'I'll come with you.'

'There's no need.'

'No. But I will, all the same.'

They pressed their way through the thronged bar to the wide exit doors which opened on to the equally sumptuous hall, where various lighted signs indicated the amenities available for guests.

The ladies' room was to the right, at the foot of the stairs which were seldom used now with the installation of the lifts. There were plenty of women, coming and going, but no sign of Tsai Pen Lung.

'Unfortunate,' remarked Damon, controlling his temper admirably, but indicating by his tone that heaven help her should he ever see her again.

Paul grimaced and turned away. 'She didn't seem that kind of creature, really. I thought she was quite likeable.'

Damon ran a hand over his hair lazily, his temper subsiding a little as he tried to find reasons for her actions. There seemed no explanation other than the one he had already come to.

A hand caught his arm, and the manager of the Royal Bay Hotel stood behind him, saying: 'I thought it was you. Mr. Thorne. A lady left this for you at reception. Is it yours?' In his hand lay the gold monogrammed lighter, with his initials inlaid with minute rubies.

Damon's eyebrows ascended in surprise. 'Yes, it's mine,' he exclaimed in bewilderment. 'Where is the lady? Has she left?'

'I believe so, sir. In any event, she asked me to make sure and give this to you personally, and apologize for walking away with it.'

Damon shook his head, taking the lighter. 'Well ... thank you,' he said, glancing in a puzzled fashion at Paul. 'Thank you.'

Much later in the evening, when he was lying in bed in the twilight area between sleeping and waking, his thoughts returned to Emma, and he realized the events of the evening had successfully banished his boredom. But his contact with the Chinese girl, beautiful though she was, had made him very aware that his feelings for Emma were still as rampant as ever, despite their differences. He tried to convince himself that his interest was purely physical, and that it would be a simple matter to make Emma submit to his demands without disturbing his peace of mind. He wanted her, and only the knowledge that she was to be his wife had caused him to control the passions she aroused in him. But now the situation was quite, quite different, and by going to Sainte Dominiquê's Cay she had placed herself at his mercy. It didn't matter that he had practically blackmailed her into it; if she was prepared to sacrifice herself for her brother, why should he care?

He rolled over restlessly on to his stomach, as his mind became too active to allow him to relax completely, automatically lifting his lighter with the case. As he lit the cigarette, he wondered why Tsai Pen Lung had left like that, without a word. Somehow it didn't tie up with her earlier desire to spend an evening in his company.

He rolled on to his back, drawing on his cigarette lazily. Had the reason she left had anything to do with her earlier nervousness, that shocked expression he had surprised on her face? Or had she merely met someone she knew, someone who might conceivably give her a more enjoyable evening, and she had been too uneasy about his reactions to come back and tell him personally?

His drifting thoughts strayed back inevitably to Emma, and he thought about the first time he had seen her. She had been seventeen at the time, young and lovely, as she still was, but with that untouched look of youth and vitality. She was an employee in the typing pool of the Thorne Chemical company's offices in Holland Park Avenue, a less imposing building which had been the London headquarters before the new block had been built. There was still a small staff at Holland Park Avenue, but even in those days Damon himself had had his head office in Cromwell Road. But this particular afternoon he had gone over to the other building to see one of his laboratory assistants who had evolved a new method of removing skin blemishes, and by parking his Aston Martin in the car-park he had almost knocked Emma down.

It was her own fault, she had freely admitted it. She was not looking where she was going, and had not been aware of the powerful car until it was almost upon her. Damon smiled as he recalled how furious he had been, and how astonished when she had turned on *him* and demanded an apology. He remembered clearly she had been wearing a scarlet pinafore dress and a white blouse with long sleeves, and she was small and dark and fiery as a cat which is suddenly attacked by a dog. Unwillingly, he had admired her spirit, knowing full well that she had no inkling of his identity.

She had remained in his thoughts all afternoon, and like some stupid lovesick youth he had been unable to get her out of his mind in the days that followed. He knew he must see her again and made discreet inquiries about her. He discovered her brother worked for him also, and after that it had been easy. He had made some excuse to invite her brother to lunch with him, and insisted he should bring his sister along too. Johnny had been only too willing to oblige, and Damon was uncaring of what the consequences might be.

Emma had not been the easiest of persons to get to know. To begin with, once she knew who he was she fought shy of seeing him, and although he could sense she was attracted to him, he was also aware of his reputation, and of the fact that Emma considered he was only playing with her as he had played with many other women. It took him several months to convince her differently, and then, just as they were being accepted together, Emma brought his world tumbling about his ears.

He could not believe it at first; would not believe it. Their relationship had been so close, so passionate, and he was only waiting a short time before he made her his wife. His public image necessitated that he should not reveal himself as an impulsive man, and he had wanted Emma to become wholly orientated with his world before making her a complete part of it. That she should expect him to accept her dismissal, just like that, was ludicrous, and he refused to believe she was serious.

But she was. Damon ground out his cigarette with renewed anger. At least they had not been officially engaged, or he would have been the laughing stock of all London. As it was, only his closest friends had known their relationship was serious, the rest, his acquaintances, accepting their break-up as just another of his affairs. He had found out that when Emma was questioned about it, she had told people he had finished with her, thus satisfying his outraged pride, and disgusting his inmost feelings.

He switched out the light now, determinedly punching his pillow into shape, and concentrating on other things. He had spent too many nights already torturing himself about Emma; he would not spend another!

CHAPTER TEN

DURING the flight from San Francisco to New York Damon and Paul were absorbed with paper work which needed to be completed before their arrival in London, and consequently it was not until the Boeing left Kennedy Airport that Damon got around to reading the papers they had bought in San Francisco and New York before their departure. The headlines of the San Francisco papers were concerned with some new world crisis, but beneath them, in less imposing print he saw: CHINESE GIRL BRUTALLY MURDERED: Second killing in four days.

Frowning, he thrust the other papers aside and read the rest of the report. It briefly outlined that a Chinese girl, as yet not identified, had been stabbed to death. Her body had been found lying on the sidewalk by a patrolling police car. There was no indication as to the location where the body had been found, and nothing to remotely connect this unknown girl with Tsai Pen Lung, and yet Damon felt an awful premonition that it was her, and that this was what she had been so afraid of.

He handed Paul the paper, pointing to the report, and saying tersely: 'What do you think of that?'

Paul read it, and then looked at Damon quizzically. 'What do you mean? Tsai Pen Lung? Don't be crazy, that would be too much of a coincidence!'

Damon shook his head. 'I don't know about that. She was scared last night. I could sense it, and then disappearing like that . . .' He sighed. 'Well, I guess it's too late now. If it is Tsai, there's nothing I can do.'

Paul lit a cigarette. 'No,' he agreed firmly. 'Don't get any mad ideas into your head of going back to identify the body. If it is Tsai, then you don't want to be involved in a murder hunt.'

Damon compressed his lips, and studied the report again moodily. He knew Paul was right, and that it was imperative that he be in London during the next couple of days to chair a meeting of the board of Thorne Chemicals, but in spite of this he felt coldly angry that anyone should be struck down and killed without any apparent motive.

He read on through the report which revealed that only four days ago another murder of this nature had taken place. This time the victim had been a man in his forties, of British nationality, which was unusual considering the enormous American population of San Francisco. The police seemed to be connecting the two crimes, and Damon plagued his mind with problems of what the two victims could possibly have had in common. He was still remote and dark-browed when the aircraft landed at London Airport, and it was with an effort he shrugged away these thoughts and began orientating himself to his new surroundings.

Emma lay on the beach beside Annabel, idly flicking through a magazine, while Annabel played with the sand. It was another glorious day, and a shady umbrella protected them from fierce glare of the afternoon sun. It was almost two months since Emma had come to Sainte Dominique, and the time was slipping away smoothly. Since Damon's departure Emma and Annabel had resumed their routine, and had got to know one another very well. They talked a lot, mostly about

Annabel's life since the accident; Emma did not seem able to penetrate Annabel's brain to the time before she was blind. Whenever she introduced this topic of conversation, Annabel would shy away from it like a startled animal, and immediately distract Emma's attention to other things.

But Emma was determined to have it out in the open, particularly as a couple of days ago she had found Annabel crying in her room during her afternoon rest. The child had refused to tell her what was the matter, but Emma had heard her murmuring the words 'Mummy, Mummy,' over and over again before she was aware of Emma's presence.

Emma had gone in search of Tansy, as she was the only one who had known Elizabeth Thorne, and from what Tansy had said, Emma had gained a clearer picture of Damon's wife.

'Och, she was a selfish creature,' exclaimed Tansy, wrinkling her nose in disgust. 'Never a minute to spare for the child unless she wanted to use her as a sword to hurt Mr. Damon.'

Emma knew she ought not to listen to this kind of kitchen gossip, but she was sure there must be a key to Annabel's blindness, something which had either caused, or assisted, the condition she now suffered. The more she learned about the accident, the less she believed in the child's injuries, for it seemed obvious her head had not been severely hurt. It was puzzling, and maybe Tansy could provide a clue.

'Where did the accident occur?' Emma asked curiously.

In Ireland,' replied Tansy grumpily. ' 'Twas a wonderful place Mr. Damon had there, but Miss Elizabeth never liked it. Too cold, and too dull, she always said.

Nothing to do, no men to amuse herself with, I suppose.' Emma's eyes widened. 'Oh, yes, there were men, lots of them,' went on Tansy, beginning to enjoy herself.

'I don't really think . . .' began Emma awkwardly.

'Och, away with you. It was common knowledge at the time. Mr. Damon knew that well enough, and I'm not saying he was any angel either. He didn't trouble himself being faithful to a bitch like her. And why should he? When she refused to care for the baby when she was born, and took herself off to London to enjoy herself.'

'I see.' Emma turned away.

'Well, would you?' asked Tansy, in disgust. 'Lord knows why she came back to Ireland when she did, causing Mr. Damon so much heartbreak over the child. They were travelling to Dublin when it happened. She was always a careless driver, had dozens of small smashes before the big one. So she was killed, and many a one of us was glad, for Mr. Damon's sake. She was no good. It was only a pity Annabel had to suffer. Still, the mercy of it is that she's still alive, for sure she takes after her father, bless her, and not that bitch she called mother.'

'Thank you,' said Emma, half smiling at the old woman. 'You've explained a lot.'

'That's good then. Now leave me be. I've got a dinner to supervise and time's pressing.'

So now Emma closed her magazine and took Annabel's hand in hers.

'Annabel,' she said softly, 'tell me about Ireland.'

Annabel stiffened and drew her hand firmly away. 'Nothing to tell,' she said abruptly. 'Can we go in the water, Emma?'

Emma compressed her lips for a moment. 'Annabel darling, we've got to discuss this some time, so it may as well be now.'

Annabel shook her head. 'I don't want to talk about it,' she said, as she had done many times before, making Emma feel self-consciously aware of what she was asking, and usually quelling her determination. But now Emma said:

'Annabel, you can't go on bottling it up. Sooner or later you've got to talk about it, so why not now? Surely you remember your home there? Did your father come often to see you? Who looked after you?'

Annabel looked mutinous, then she sighed. 'Yes, Daddy came often,' she admitted quietly. 'And Tansy took care of me, and I had children to play with. It was wonderful,' she sounded wistful.

Emma twisted her fingers together. 'And your mother?' she said.

Annabel bent her head. 'Elizabeth?'

'Yes.'

'She told me to call her that. She didn't like being called Mummy. She said it made her feel old.'

Emma crossed her fingers. At last Annabel was volunteering information.

'Did you see a lot of your mummy?'

Annabel chewed her lips and shook her head.

Emma tried another approach. 'Did you want her to be there a lot?'

Annabel rose to her feet. 'Can we go swimming?' she asked.

Emma sighed, and rose too, shedding her towelling bathrobe.

'I suppose so,' she said, realizing it would take longer than an overnight success to get the true story out of

Annabel.

After dinner that evening, when Annabel was fast asleep, and Louisa was sewing in the lounge. Emma went for a walk along the beach. It was wonderful, out in the cool air after the heat of the day. She had showered before dinner, but her body still felt hot and she thought she would shower again before she went to bed.

The water lapped invitingly on the sand, soothing and scented with the perfumes of the flowers that soaked the atmosphere during the long days. Clusters of palms rustled in the breeze, and the strange sounds of the night-waking animals provided a background of clicking and chattering and soft whispering among the undergrowth.

A streak of colour on the sand startled her for a moment, until she realized it was the huge beach towel which she and Annabel had been using that afternoon. She shook it out gently, and folded it under her arm. It was then that the idea struck her. She would take a dip in the sea, instead of waiting until she got back to the house. The water was never cold and the prospect of a solitary swim was very appealing. That she had no bathing suit to wear did not daunt her. The beach was always deserted, the villagers using the more shingled beach where the boats were drawn up. It was always accepted that the beach below the house was private. It would be a simple matter to dry herself after her swim on the towel, and then slide back into her underclothes and the slim-fitting Terylene dress she was wearing.

The water creamed over her limbs like liquid satin, and as she had never swum in the nude before it was a tantalizing experience. It was wonderful to glide smoothly through the water, the moon gilding the skins of the multi-coloured fish that swam hastily past her, as though afraid of her. She did not swim out very far. She had no desire to get into difficulties in her situation, and she smiled to herself at her thoughts. She felt relaxed, and contented, and could even partially convince herself that without Damon's presence she could dispel the nagging loneliness she felt when he was around.

At last she waded up out of the water, and lifting the towel wrapped it right round her and began to dry herself. She felt much cooler now and quite refreshed.

When the undergrowth crunched ominously near her, she almost jumped out of her skin. With trembling fingers she wrapped the towel tight around her, sarong-wise, and stared expectantly into the darkness.

'Who's there?' she challenged in a shaky voice.

The bushes parted, and a tall, broad, dark man stepped into the clearing, looking broodingly attractive in the pale light of the moon.

'You!' she exclaimed in astonishment. 'When did you arrive?'

Damon shrugged his broad shoulders. 'About fifteen minutes ago. Louisa told me where you were. She was concerned because you were so long. I said I would find you.'

Emma clenched her fingers tightly on the top of the towel, and he looked annoyed.

'What are you wearing under that thing?' he asked angrily. 'Good God! You surely haven't been swimming *like that*, alone!'

Emma's face turned a deep red. 'Why not?'

'Good heavens, you don't need me to tell you that!' He strode across to her furiously. 'Anyone might have come upon you, do you realize that? And what possible chance would you have had if some drunken clod had taken it into his head to rape you?' His voice was stingingly violent.

Emma looked up at him, albeit a little nervously. 'No one came. Except you, of course!'

'And you trust me,' he muttered savagely.

'Shouldn't I?' she asked quietly.

'No, damn you, you shouldn't!'

'Why? What are you going to do? Strip the towel off me? Would that amuse you?' She was deliberately taunting him, his anger triggering off some crazy provocation inside herself.

'No, it would not *amuse* me,' he said tautly.

Emma felt her senses reeling at the tone of his voice. She had to force herself to remember that he hated her and despised her, and that anything he might say to her would be said to hurt and humiliate her even more than he had done so already.

She turned away to pick up her clothes, and stumbled over the ends of the towel. It tugged at the insecure fastening she had made under her arm and by hastily trying to secure it again, she lost her balance and fell ignominiously on the sand at his feet. Feeling ridiculously like a schoolgirl, caught out in some childish prank, she rolled over and looked up at him. He looked so big standing over her like that, and she quickly scrambled to her feet, tucking the towel back into place.

'If you'll excuse me, I'll get dressed,' she murmured self-consciously, aware that her wet hair must be clinging in strands to her neck, and she must look an absolute mess. He looked so cool and distant, his suit dark blue and expensively tailored, his shirt contrasting brilliantly with the darkness of his neck.

His hard fingers suddenly encircled her wrist, preventing her from moving away. His eyes looked hard and cynical, as he said:

'No. I like you as you are.'

Emma's heart began to thump, and she tried unsuccessfully to prise his fingers from her wrist with her other hand. He seemed amused at her paltry efforts, and it infuriated her.

With deliberately slow movements he pulled her close against him, the fluffiness of the towel clinging to his dark suit. Emma thought inconsequently that he could afford to ruin his clothes, no matter now expensive they might be.

'I'm wet,' she protested breathlessly, turning her head to one side, refusing to look at him.

'Interesting,' he murmured lazily, his mouth seeking the curve of her neck.

'Damon, *please*,' she begged, trying to hold on to her emotions.

'Please what?' he asked mockingly, caressing her bare shoulder.

'Let me go!'

'Why should I? If it amuses me to make love to you, why shouldn't I do so? Since I've been away I've realized that physically you still attract me; you're a very attractive creature, you always were.'

'Damon,' she pleaded, 'don't be like this!'

He smiled, but it was not a pleasant smile. 'Why? What can you do to stop me? If I let you go now, there's nothing to stop me from taking you at some other time, is there?'

Emma turned to look at him, unable to prevent the surge of love and compassion he aroused in her. If she hadn't known about Elizabeth she would have said she had hurt him more than she had thought possible. The expression on her face must have been easy for him to read, for he said:

'Dear God! Don't look at me like that!' His hands dropped from her, and he turned away, disgusted with himself.

Emma linked her hands together nervously. Now that she was free she found she didn't want to go. It didn't seem to matter any more what his reasons were for touching her, she only knew she needed him now more than at any other time of her life. The love she had felt for him when she was seventeen had increased instead of dying as she had hoped it would, and today she loved him as the woman she was.

He brushed his suit down carelessly and said: 'Come back to the house, as soon as you're dressed.'

'Damon,' she murmured tentatively.

'Don't speak to me,' he muttered roughly.

'Damon, don't be like that!'

He swung on her savagely, his face pale beneath his tan.

'Like what?' he muttered violently. 'Don't be deceived, Emma! I didn't let you go because I felt sorry for you. I let you go because I have no intention of losing my own self-respect over a little cheat like you!'

Emma stepped back a pace, a hand to her mouth in horror.

'Does that hurt you?' he taunted mockingly. 'Good. I'd hate to think we misunderstood each other.'

'There's no danger of that now,' said Emma, picking up her clothes, and running swiftly away towards the house without waiting to dress.

CHAPTER ELEVEN

EMMA discovered that Damon was alone this time. He had left Paul in London to handle his affairs, and had flown to Nassau and come on from there by launch instead of by helicopter, and that accounted for the fact that she had not heard him arrive.

Despite their quarrel on the night of his arrival, she found he had no intention of neglecting Annabel this visit, and Emma's presence, insisted upon by his daughter, was something he and Emma had to put up with.

If Emma had felt any heartache when she came to the island it was nothing compared to the way she felt now, and she thought that Damon had succeeded in his mission to make her suffer for her actions in the past. She thought he must be feeling very pleased with himself, that he should have hurt her this way, and she despised herself for allowing it to happen.

She wondered if she would have the opportunity while he was here to talk to him about Annabel's mother. It was not a prospect she looked forward to, but she felt it was a necessary adjunct to Annabel's recovery.

Her chance came one afternoon while Annabel was resting, Louisa had gone into Nassau for the day, and apart from Tansy they were alone. Not that Tansy ever intruded. She was usually to be found in the kitchen knitting or sewing, making interminable little garments for the children in the village.

Damon was in his study, working, and when the house was quiet Emma made her way there and knocked softly on the door.

At Damon's command she entered, and closed the door behind her. Damon looked up, his eyes showing surprise when he saw who it was.

'Well?' he said uncompromisingly.

Emma sighed and said: 'I want to talk to you about Annabel.'

'Again?'

'Yes, again. Not about you, though. I want to talk to you about the accident.'

Damon's eyes grew guarded. 'Yes? What about the accident? Surely that needn't concern you. Your duties here are to look after Annabel during the times when she needs a companion. That you're a nurse yourself doesn't necessarily imply that you should interest yourself in the closer details of her case history.'

'Yes, I'm a nurse,' exclaimed Emma hotly, 'and I think I have a right to talk to you about the accident, whatever my duties are here. Oh, I know I'm just a glorified nanny, and I know my qualifications had nothing to do with your reasons for bringing me here, but now that I am here I have no intention of allowing you to treat me like an imbecile. I know a little bit about this and I don't think an operation is what Annabel needs. I think her blindness is a mental, rather than a physical, blockage.'

Damon lay back in his seat cynically regarding her. 'Oh, really? So you know that, do you?'

'I don't *know* it, I feel it. Damon, for goodness' sake, doctors can only work on the knowledge that's revealed to them. Surely, if they didn't know the facts of the relationship between you and Annabel's mother they would have no idea of the worries and anxieties that child might be nursing . . .'

Damon sprang angrily to his feet. 'Just what the hell

do you mean by that?'

Emma flushed. 'You know perfectly well what I mean,' she asserted firmly.

'Indeed! And who's been regaling you with information about my relations with my wife? Tansy, I suppose, the old gossip!'

'Tansy won't have a word said against you,' retorted Emma swiftly. 'Anything she's told me doesn't in any way impinge upon your good character!'

'And that's supposed to placate me, I suppose!' His eye flashed brilliantly. 'Why don't you mind your own business?'

Emma would not be intimidated. 'Annabel is my business. If your marital relations reflect on her illness, I think I have a right to try and lift that blockage whatever it is.'

'My marital relations, as you call them, couldn't have been worse,' he said sardonically. 'There; does that answer you?'

Emma's face deepened with colour. This was embarrassing her far more than it was embarrassing him.

'Then why . . .?' Emma had to bite back the question, but he looked at her intently, as though aware of what that question would have been.

'Why did I marry her?' he asked. 'That was what you were going to say, wasn't it?'

Emma bent her head. 'Am I so transparent?'

'To me, in some ways, yes.'

She looked up at him. 'Then . . . ?' She sighed. 'You didn't find it so difficult to forget me, Damon. You're making me stay here to atone for not marrying you, and yet as far as I can see I broke no hearts!'

Damon's face darkened. 'I loved you, Emma!' he muttered savagely.

129

'Did you? Or was it your pride I damaged? You couldn't believe that anyone would turn you, Damon Thorne, down!' Her voice was bitter.

Damon caught her roughly by the shoulders, his hard fingers bruising the soft flesh of her shoulders.

'Don't dare speak to me like that!' he exclaimed furiously. 'I said I loved you, and I did. You were the only woman I ever loved, or ever wanted to marry.'

She stared at him uncomprehendingly. 'But you married Elizabeth!' she said incredulously. 'Only ten weeks after . . .' Her voice trailed away.

'Yes, I married Elizabeth. I'm not denying that, am I?'

'No. But . . . but . . . Annabel . . .'

Damon's eyes narrowed with derison. 'Don't be naïve,' he said cruelly. 'She was my wife, we shared the same bed!'

'Oh, Damon!' she whispered achingly, at last understanding why he had married Elizabeth. He had been hurt, so hurt, that he had done a crazy thing like that without caring of the consequences.

'Don't pity me,' he exclaimed coldly. 'I knew what I was doing.'

Emma shook her head, and pressed the palms of her hands against her hot cheeks. 'I'm sorry, Damon.'

'Are you?' His voice was harsh. 'How touching! Or perhaps you see me now as a meal ticket for life, something which didn't seem so important seven years ago!'

Emma's eyes widened in horror at the callousness of his words, and goaded beyond endurance she slapped his face, and turned quickly away towards the door. But Damon forestalled her, moving swiftly for such a big man, and he lay back against the door preventing her from making her escape.

She saw the tell-tale line of her fingermarks appearing along his cheek, and saw the dangerous expression in his dark eyes.

'No one slaps my face and gets away with it,' he muttered angrily, and straightening up he pulled her across to him, close against the warm hardness of his body. She felt his hands sliding the scoop neckline of her dress from her shoulders, and then the burning passion of his mouth against her flesh.

'Oh, God,' he murmured thickly, 'I want you, Emma!'

Emma tried not to respond, but when his mouth found hers, her lips parted helplessly, and surrendering to sensual enjoyment, she wound her bare arms about his neck, and kissed him back.

It wasn't like the other time he had kissed her, when his sole desire had been to hurt her. This time it was a mutual mounting of passion, and Emma didn't want him to stop. At one point Damon would have drawn back as his innate decency asserted itself, but Emma would not let him go, and his heightened senses would not let him resist.

And then, without warning, the study door opened, and Christopher Thorne stood in the doorway, staring at them in amazement. Emma came immediately to her senses, but Damon was slower to release her, his eyes still a little glazed from his emotions.

'Well, well,' said Chris dryly. 'I'm afraid I've made a complete ass of myself, haven't I? You should hang a "*Do not disturb*" notice on the door, Damon.'

Damon pushed Emma reluctantly away from him, and shook his head.

'I need a drink,' he muttered, turning towards the

tray of drinks on a side table.

'Make that two,' remarked Chris amiably, turning to look at Emma, who was smoothing her hair and her dress, and feeling terribly embarrassed.

'Calm down, kid,' he said kindly. 'I know how you must feel.' He grinned, and glanced at Damon. 'No wonder he was so mad when I detained you in Nassau!'

Damon came back, and handed Chris a whisky and Emma a glass of lime and lemon. Then he helped himself to a liberal amount of Scotch, and flung himself into a low armchair near his desk. Emma marvelled at his composure. She could hardly believe that less than five minutes before he had been at the mercy of his emotions. He looked very attractive in close-fitting charcoal grey pants and a navy blue knitted nylon shirt, open at the neck, and she ran a hand up her forehead, feeling how damp it had become. Damon's eyes met hers for a moment, then he said, to Chris:

'What brings you here?'

Chris shrugged. 'This and that. We haven't seen much of you since you got back, and Helen thought you might like to come over this evening for a meal.'

Damon shrugged lazily. 'Thanks, but I don't think I will,' he said, 'I'm still behind with some of this correspondence. I thought I might get some of it done after dinner.'

Chris glanced pointedly at Emma. 'Is that so?'

Damon's eyes were cynical. 'Please, Chris, skip the humour!'

Chris smiled. 'Why? It's all a guy can do in circumstances like these. Well, anyway, if you're too busy how about letting Emma come with me? I'd see she got back safely.'

'I think not,' said Damon, reaching for a cigarette, before Emma had the chance to reply for herself.

Emma sipped her drink, hardly aware of their conversation. She was glad Damon was there to make her decisions for her. At the moment she felt as though she had no will of her own.

Chris grimaced and finished his drink. 'Okay, okay. So I've had a wasted journey.'

Damon roused himself apologetically. 'I'm sorry, Chris. Just don't ever do that to me again, will you?'

'That's a promise,' remarked Chris sardonically. 'Coming to see me off, Emma?'

Emma shook her head, and shrugging, Chris went out giving them a regretful smile.

After he had gone, Emma finished her drink hastily and said:

'Annabel will be waking up soon. I'd better go and see her.'

Damon rose to his feet but did not touch her, 'All right,' he said moodily. He ran a hand round the back of his neck. 'I guess I should apologize to you too, shouldn't I?'

Emma shook her head, looking down at the toes of her sandals.

'What do you mean, no?' he asked, softly but violently. 'You know perfectly well that if Chris hadn't arrived as he did . . .' He shook his head. 'I couldn't have stopped myself, and I somehow don't think you could have, either.'

Emma flushed.

'I don't usually lose control of myself; in fact when we were . . . together . . . before, I never allowed us to reach that point. But just now I didn't particularly care about your feelings; I guess the animal in me took over.' He gripped the back of his neck with one hand flexing his muscles tiredly. 'I disgust myself!' he muttered angrily. 'I thought I could hurt you that way, but I was wrong.'

Emma linked her hands together tightly. 'Don't blame yourself,' she said, 'I asked for it. I behaved like a bitch, but I didn't want you to stop!'

Damon's eyes were enigmatical. 'I can hardly believe that. Once you had the chance, and turned me down, *flat.*'

'Because of you!' she said wearily. 'Only because of you.'

His eyes narrowed. 'Because of me?' he echoed. 'What story is this you've dreamed up?'

'It's no story. It's the truth.' Emma turned away. 'Oh, what's the use? You'll never believe me.'

'Try me.'

'It's too hard to explain. It sounds trifling now, but at the time it seemed the most important thing in the world.'

'Go on.'

Emma sighed, casting about in her mind for words to explain her actions.

'Do you remember that dinner party you gave, when you invited Lord and Lady Masterham?'

Damon frowned. 'Well, I remember them, I don't say I remember any particular dinner party, why?'

'Well, after dinner when you and her husband were having drinks, Lady Masterham and I sat out on the balcony. She started off by telling me how clever you were, and how successful you were in business, and how important it was for a man in your position to have the right wife. She said she thought you were terribly courageous becoming involved with a little nobody like me, when I had no money or position, as well as being far too young for you. She said it was completely out of character and she hoped our affair wouldn't have an adverse influence on your position and so on.' Emma hunched her shoulders. 'You can guess the rest, can't you? And she wasn't the only one by any means. All your so-called friends thought I would ruin your life, spoil everything for you. I knew you would never believe that. Besides, I knew we loved one another.' She bent her head. 'But I was young and afraid that what they said might be true, and I loved you too much to want to ruin your life. So I pretended there was someone else. I knew if I told you the truth, you would never let me go, so the way I took was the only way. But when you married Elizabeth Kingsford just that short while later, and then produced a daughter, I thought I should *die*!' She looked up at him, hardly daring to face the expression on his face and see the disbelief in his eyes.

Damon was standing, as though mesmerized. With an effort he roused himself and said:

'Is this true?' His voice was harsh. 'You're not just making it up?'

Emma shook her head. 'No, I'm not making it up.'

Damon reached for her hand, and slid his fingers lingeringly up her arm. 'You must have been crazy,' he muttered savagely. 'Did you think I'd give a damn what anybody thought?'

'I knew you wouldn't,' exclaimed Emma. 'Don't you see? That's why I had to lie to you or you would never have let me do it.'

'That's for sure,' he muttered incredulously. 'But why wait until now to tell me?'

Emma lifted her shoulders in a helpless gesture. 'I suppose I couldn't stand your torturing yourself, and me, any longer. You had to know the truth.'

Damon shook his head bewilderedly. 'Oh, Emma, what a little fool you've been, wasting all these years!'

'They've not been wasted,' said Emma, attempting to regain her composure. 'Oh, I know my pride wouldn't let me go on having you think me such a selfish, stupid creature, deserving of your hatred and disgust, but the situation hasn't really changed. We're older now, both of us, but I'm still a nobody without a penny to my name, and you're still the chairman of Thorne Chemicals.'

Damon's fingers suddenly hurt her arm. 'What am I supposed to glean from that remark?' he asked tersely.

'Just what I said,' replied Emma wearily. 'I can't marry you, Damon, no more now than I could then.'

Damon's eyes were incredulous. 'Casting aside the unnecessary comment that I haven't asked you, would you mind telling me why?'

'You know why.' Emma moved restlessly. 'Damon, Elizabeth Kingsford wasn't like me. She had money, and position in society; your marriage to her was at least a suitable one.'

'And look how successful that turned out,' Damon ground out angrily. 'We lived together for exactly three months; all the rest was hell!'

'Well, maybe she was all wrong for you. From what Tansy has said I should think she was the complete antithesis of yourself.'

Damon released her abruptly, stubbing out his cigarette and picking a cigar out of the box on his desk. 'What would you suggest I do?' he asked bitterly. 'Find a woman I could live with, and have you, or Tansy, vet her to see if she's suitable!'

136

Emma clenched her fists. 'Are you thinking of marrying again?'

'I may do,' he murmured sardonically, his only desire to hurt her again.

'Oh, Damon!' she cried, and turning, she ran swiftly out of the room as she had done before.

CHAPTER TWELVE

THE next morning brought a letter from Johnny. It was longer than the usual short notes he had been sending her, and Emma took it gratefully, glad of something to take her mind off Damon, and the eventual outcome of their association.

But when she read the letter she found that the reason for its length was purely a selfish one. Johnny was in trouble again. He needed money. Could she let him have a hundred and seventy-five pounds?

Emma shook her head in astonishment. She would have thought Johnny's experience a short while ago would have taught him a salutary lesson, but as it was he seemed to have become more embroiled in deceit than ever, and was in an even worse predicament now than before.

She didn't know what to do. It would not be difficult to contact her bank in London and have them make out a cheque for Johnny to cover his needs, but what then? Her bank balance was not a large one, using so much as she had to keep both herself and Johnny in food and clothing when she had been working at the hospital. Johnny had borrowed money carelessly from her, and had never made much contribution towards their joint budget, and if she were now to be expected to foot all his gambling debts she would soon have nothing at all. She wished there was someone she could turn to, someone with whom she could discuss her problems. But there was no one. She had no intention of speaking to Damon about it, for although she felt sure he would despise

Johnny, nevertheless he would see that the money was paid somehow, perhaps exacting more payment from her in return.

Then she shook her head. That was less than honest. Damon had proved himself an honourable man, and she had no cause to think otherwise. So the problem remained hers, and with a sigh of dejection she wrote the letter to the bank in London authorizing them to pay Johnny a hundred and seventy-five pounds.

London seemed so far away somehow, but Johnny's problems bridged the gulf between them, enmeshing her in his web of dishonesty. Three or four months ago she wouldn't have believed Johnny could behave in such a fashion, but it was remarkable how the mind adjusted itself, so that now she accepted it in much the same way she accepted her own unhappy position here.

Later the same day, Damon had a telephone call from Paul in London. He was lying on an airbed beside the swimming pool with Annabel when Rosa came to call him to the phone. Expecting some problem over business, Damon was surprised when Paul said:

'The apartment was broken into last night!'

Roused fully now from his lethargy, Damon's voice was curt. 'The apartment?' he muttered. 'What the hell was Baines doing?'

Baines was his manservant who lived at the London penthouse.

'Baines was coshed, and tied up,' replied Paul, 'he's in a pretty bad way. I guess you could say it was touch and go.'

'Good God!' Damon was astounded. 'Well . . . what did they take? The Monet? Or the Renoir?'

'Neither, curiously enough. Nothing was actually

stolen. The whole place was turned over; what a shambles! But that was all! At a guess I'd say they were looking for something.'

Damon ran a hand round the back of his neck, frowning deeply. He was silent for so long that Paul said:

'Are you still there?'

Sure, sure! I was trying to think, that's all.' Damon shook his head incredulously. 'I can't understand it. Can you?'

'No. That's for sure.' Paul sounded half amused. 'Anyway, I'm ringing from the apartment now. The police are here, of course. I called them as soon as I found Baines.'

'You found Baines?'

'Yes. I came round early this morning, could get no reply, so I used the key you left. It was pretty ghastly finding Baines like that. He'd lost a lot of blood, but he's had a transfusion now and the doctors say he should pull through.'

'Thank God for that,' said Damon fervently. 'Poor old Baines. How did they get in?'

'I guess he opened the door to them. There was no sign of a struggle and of course no windows had been tampered with. After all, he had no reason not to answer the door.'

'That's right.' Damon sighed heavily. 'Still, I wish we knew what it was all about. What took you so long to ring me?'

'Oh, you know, the usual police routine; proving my identity and so on, and then actually getting the call. Anyway, is there anything you want me to do? I'll get the place straightened out of course, but after that, what?'

Damon shrugged. 'I don't know. I guess you could

sleep at the apartment if you wanted to.' He smiled to himself. 'Don't think I want you to get coshed, Paul, but if they turned the place over I should presume the safest place in London right now is my apartment, get it?'

'You think they might try my place?' Paul was incredulous. He had a flat not far from Damon's apartment.

'Who knows? We don't know what, if anything, they were searching for, but if it's anything to do with the company, they're bound to know you're my personal assistant, and who knows what they might do.'

'Okay, okay,' said Paul hurriedly. 'You've convinced me. I'll sleep at the apartment, and I'll keep the alarm system on day and night. You can call me a coward if you like, but I'm taking no chances.'

Damon's tension released itself a little and he laughed. 'Good man! And don't worry! I'll be back in a few days myself.'

But after Paul had rung off, Damon felt the tension returning. Who would want to turn out his apartment? And why should anyone do so without taking advantage of the small fortune in paintings and ivory? Even a common thief who was searching for some particular object would be tempted to take something for his trouble. The only alternative was that whoever had turned over the apartment had been acting under orders from someone else with strict instructions that nothing incriminating should be taken.

He walked slowly outside, lighting a cigar thoughtfully. It was a problem which defied analysis; a contradiction from start to finish.

Annabel, hearing his approach, said, 'What's wrong, Daddy?'

Damon stared at her. The child was too sensitive by

half. She could tell in some strange way that he was disturbed.

'Why, nothing, Annabella,' he lied smoothly. 'Come along. We'll swim for a while, then Daddy has some work to do.'

Emma spent the day alternately worrying about Johnny and worrying about her own situation here. She did not see Damon all day, avoiding the swimming pool when she knew he was there with Annabel. The weather didn't help either. It was very warm, and there were ominous black clouds in the distance which heralded a storm. But the storm didn't come, and somehow Emma wished it would. At least it would give her something else to think about.

The next day dawned heavy and enervating. There was no sun and the clouds were closer now, sharply defined against the yellow-coloured sky. Louisa left after breakfast for Nassau. It was her day off, and Joseph was taking her to Nassau for a day's shopping. She had invited Emma to go with her knowing full well that the girl was entitled to some free time, but Emma refused to go, making some excuse about the weather and the fact that she had a slight headache. Contrarily, after Louisa had gone, Emma wished she had accompanied her, for with Damon at home Annabel had no time for anyone else.

However, after breakfast Damon told Annabel he had some telephoning to do and consequently the child came in search of Emma. They went down to the beach, taking a story book along, and Emma read several short stories to Annabel before Annabel said:

'Let's not read any more, Emma. Tell me about when you were a little girl. Did you have a mummy and a daddy? Did you have brothers and sisters?'

Emma sighed and closed the book. 'Yes,' she said, slowly. 'I had a mummy and a daddy. But I have only one brother. There were just the four of us. But we were very happy. We didn't have a lot of money like your daddy, but that didn't seem to matter. We used to be able to afford a holiday at the seaside every year, and really that's all the travelling we ever did.'

Annabel digested this. 'Was your house big?' she asked.

'Oh, no!' Emma smiled. 'There were three bedrooms and one bathroom. Then a couple of rooms and a kitchen downstairs.'

'Is that all?' Annabel was obviously surprised. Her experience of houses had been limited to huge villas and country houses like the house her father had owned in Ireland.

'Yes, that's all,' said Emma, sighing. 'That's more than a lot of people have, Annabel. You're a terribly lucky little girl having a lovely home, and a swimming pool, and anything your heart desires.'

'I'm not lucky,' exclaimed Annabel, at once. 'Oh, I love Daddy, and I'm sure he loves me, but I'd give everything else up if I could have a real home and a mummy and daddy who loved one another and baby brothers and sisters.' She clasped her hands round her drawn-up knees. 'Oh, I'd love to have lots of children in the house, and babies for me to look after, instead of only Patricia!'

Emma felt a lump in her throat. In her own emotional state Annabel's words were too sharp, too piercing, too desirable to be considered.

'Sometimes it happens,' Emma said slowly, 'that two people who get married find that they just can't live together. It's not their fault, it's not anybody's fault. They just can't get along. Then when that happens, if there are any children, it makes it unpleasant for them. Which is unfortunate!'

'But they oughtn't to have children, then,' exclaimed Annabel, tears springing to her eyes.'

'Children are not always . . .' Emma sought about in her mind for a way to describe what she wanted to say; 'Annabel, you must try and understand, when your father married your mother they had you before they realized their mistake. Do you see?' She bit her lip. 'Be thankful that at least you have one parent who thinks the world of you.'

Annabel buried her face in her hands suddenly. 'Oh, Emma,' she sobbed passionately, 'I was going to hurt Daddy. He loved me, but I was going away. I was going to leave him.' She sobbed bitterly.

Emma frowned, and then, stroking Annabel's head gently, she said:

'Leave him? What on earth are you talking about?'

Annabel raised a tear-stained face. 'You don't understand, Emma. It was when . . . when . . . when the accident happened!' She hid her face again.

'Go on.' Emma's frown deepened.

'I can't. I can't. Oh, I'm so ashamed!'

Emma shook her gently. 'Annabel, listen, this is me, Emma! You can tell me. I won't be angry, or shocked. Won't you please tell me?'

Annabel raised her face again. 'Do you promise?'

'Of course.'

'All right, then.' Annabel rubbed her cheeks dry with her fingers. 'Mummy came to the house that day, the day of the accident. I hadn't seen her for months, and I hadn't seen Daddy for weeks. She . . . she told me that

Daddy had stopped her coming to see me, that he didn't really love me or he wouldn't leave me like he had. She said she loved me. She said she wanted to take me away and make a home for me in England. I said no. I said I didn't want to leave Daddy anyway, but she said I was stupid.'

Emma's fist clenched. Elizabeth's methods of persuasion were heartless against a four-year-old.

'Well, when I wouldn't go with her she started to tell me what she would give me.' Annabel's lip trembled. 'For months I'd wanted a pony, but Daddy said I was too young, that it would be dangerous for me. When Elizabeth started telling me what I could have I asked if I could have a pony, and she said of course, I could have two if I wanted. So I said I would go with her. She didn't let me pack any of my things. She said we would get all new ones, so's not to make anybody suspicious about us going together. I took Patricia, that's all.' She stopped, her eyes streaming with tears. 'The . . . then the accident happened and Elizabeth was killed, and I was so unhappy, and so ashamed. I . . . I couldn't tell Daddy what I'd been going to do. I couldn't tell him that I'd gone for the pony, you see!' And Annabel lapsed into uncontrollable sobbing.

But Emma felt a surge of hope inside her. If what Annabel had told her was true then there was every reason to believe that her blindness was indeed a mental blockage. Poor Annabel, unable to face her father; to see the disappointment in his face when he found out the truth; not wanting to *see*!

But for the present Emma comforted her, and soothed her and dried her eyes, then helped her back to the house for lunch.

After lunch when Annabel was settled for her rest,

Emma wandered outside and seated herself beside the swimming pool mulling over in her mind everything Annabel had said. It was true that she had discovered a motive for Annabel's blockage, and a reason behind her refusal to talk about the accident. But was it enough? And now she had found it, what could be done about it? She doubted whether the fact of Damon knowing the truth would miraculously return Annabel's sight to her.

She lit a cigarette and sighed deeply, her thoughts turning to Johnny and his problems. She had sent him a cable telling him that she had also contacted her bank and authorized them to pay him the money, but she wondered whether she had done the right thing. Even if this solved Johnny's immediate problems, the future looked bleak indeed.

And how much longer would she be allowed to remain here? Now that Damon knew the whole story he had no reason for keeping her on Sainte Dominique. She had no positive way of knowing what his real feelings were towards her. He still desired her, she attracted him physically, but he had never mentioned love. And even if the miracle happened and he did still love her enough to marry her, she had successfully cut the ground from under his feet. It was no good; she couldn't bring herself to believe that their marriage would work, any more than his marriage with Elizabeth had worked. She knew nothing of his world, of the life he led. As chairman of the Thorne combine he had duties to perform, social gatherings to attend; he needed someone who was smart and witty, sophisticated and worldly, not someone like herself who really only wanted a home and children. She loved him, there was no doubt about that, but she could not believe that his feelings for her, strong though they might be at the moment, could survive for long after his complete possession of her physically. She merely intrigued him because she was, as yet, untouched.

She smoothed her cheeks with the palms of her hands. Where was it all going to end?

She heard the soft tread of footsteps across the lawn, and glanced round nervously. Damon approached her, looking broad and attractive in narrow-fitting navy blue pants and a dark red knitted shirt. He reached her side, and seated himself in the adjoining lounger. He drew on a cigar, and then said:

'Where have you been the last couple of days?'

Emma shrugged, her cheeks burning. 'Around,' she said.

'Avoiding me,' he muttered angrily, his eyes flashing.

'No . . . that is . . . you've been looking after Annabel. I've been catching up on some mending.'

'Come on, come on! What do you take me for? I can read you like a book, Emma. You've been avoiding me like the plague. What's the matter? Are you afraid I might turn on you? Or do you think that now that I know the truth I might pester you to marry me?'

'Stop it!' Emma's words were torn from her. 'Stop it!'

'Why?' Damon studied his cigar moodily, and then stubbed it out. 'Anyway, I have to go back to London tomorrow. Then you'll be able to relax again. Is there any message you would like me to give Johnny?'

Emma twisted her hands together. 'You . . . you haven't stayed very long.'

'No.' Damon shrugged. 'Oh, well, if you must know I had a call from Paul yesterday. The apartment was searched a couple of nights ago, and Baines was coshed and nearly killed.'

Emma's eyes widened. 'Baines,' she echoed. 'Oh, how awful!'

'Yes. Anyway, nothing was stolen, so I suppose I should be thankful for small mercies.'

'Then why ... ?'

He shrugged. 'You know as much as me. We can't understand it and the police can't understand it, so I guess I'll have to go back and try and find out what gives.'

'Oh, Damon!' Emma stared at him. 'Must you go?' Then, as though realizing the betraying tone of her words, she continued: 'I mean, you will be careful, won't you?'

Damon's fingers encircled her wrist. 'Emma,' he muttered, 'please, Emma, what do you want me to do?' His face was pale under the tan and Emma felt her bones turning to water at his touch. 'Don't *do* this to us!'

'Damon—' she began, shaking her head. His eyes burned her up, and she felt the strength of his emotions enveloping her. 'You must go to London ...'

'I'm not talking about London,' he muttered heavily, 'and you know it! This is *us*! Our lives! And you're destroying me!'

'Oh, Damon,' she whispered brokenly.

'You love me, damn you, I know you do!' he swore violently.

Emma's eyes were drenched with unshed tears as she looked at him. Gone was the arrogant tycoon she had grown so used to seeing, this was just Damon, on his knees beside her chair, his hands gripping her arms, his eyes tortured with longing which she at last accepted only she could assuage for some incomprehensible reason.

'Yes, yes, yes,' she cried, unable to deny him anything. 'Of course I love you, I always have. Damon, I want to give you your life, not to destroy it!'

'Then love me,' he muttered harshly, 'just love me!' He bent his head, putting his mouth to the palms of her hands. 'Because, God help me, I can't live without you any longer!'

Emma could hardly believe that this was actually happening. It was like coming through a dark tunnel into sunlight, and she had to shake herself to assure herself that she wasn't dreaming. Maybe later doubts would return, but just at this moment there was no one but Damon and herself, and this wonderful thing between them.

She slid off the chair into his arms compulsively, falling beside him on the grass, feeling the warmth of his body engulfing her.

'Oh, darling,' he groaned, his mouth caressing her eyes and ears passionately. Emma's arms were around his neck drawing him closer. It was no good, she couldn't fight him any longer, not when she wanted to give in so badly.

It seemed aeons later when Damon finally rolled on to his back, his hand still holding her wrist so that she could not escape from him even had she wanted to. He sought about for his cigarette case and extracting a cigarette he put it between his lips and drew out his lighter. As he did so his mind inconsequently sprang back in time to San Francisco, and Tsai Pen Lung. The lighter seemed significant somehow, and a faint frown crossed his face. He ought to have discovered who the Chinese girl had been who had been murdered that last night they were in the States.

Emma, who propped herself up on one elbow, saw the

frown, and looked down at him anxiously.

'Damon,' she murmured questioningly. 'You're not
... you're not regretting it already?'

Damon slid the lighter back into his pocket, and
shook his head, a lazy smile flickering over his face. He
put up his free hand and caressed the nape of her neck
gently.

'Now what do you think?' he murmured huskily.
'Emma, I love you. I adore you. I *worship* you! I've
always loved you, even when I hated you ... and make
no mistake about it, I did hate you!'

'And now?'

'And now we're going to be married, no matter how
many protestations you can raise. I'm losing the desire
to spend my life in a boardroom. I want more free time,
I want children ... our children.'

'And Annabel?' murmured Emma, allowing him to
draw her head down to his chest, where she lay con-
tentedly, at peace for the first time in years.

Damon blew the smoke from his cigarette lazily into
the air.

'Annabel is fond of you already. She's proved that. I
don't think she'll find the transition from friend to step-
mother so hard to bear. Besides, you'll be more of a
mother to her than Elizabeth ever was.'

'Oh, yes!' Emma sat up. 'That reminds me, I found
something out today. Elizabeth was taking Annabel
away from you when the accident occurred.'

Damon nodded. 'I guessed that.'

Emma sighed. 'Well, Annabel doesn't know. She is
harbouring some terrible self-recriminations concerning
that day.' She looked down at him seriously. 'I really
think it might have something to do with her blindness.'

Damon's eyes widened a moment, and then he sighed. 'But why? I mean ... she knows I wouldn't blame her for anything that happened that day.'

'I know. But don't you see, it's you she's concerned about, not herself.' Emma spread wide her hands. 'Darling, she blames herself for allowing Elizabeth to talk her into going. She feels guilty about leaving you!'

Damon carried one of her hands to his lips thoughtfully. 'And you really think this might cause her condition?'

'Well, it might have something to do with it. If we could make her believe you don't care what she did, and you still love her just as much as ever in spite of it ... well, she might be on the road to recovery. Then the specialists might be able to shake her muscles out of their inertia.'

Damon sat up too now. 'If only they could!' he muttered fervently.

Emma suddenly slid her arms round him, hugging him close, still hardly able to believe they were at peace with one another.

'Emma,' he groaned, a little half-heartedly, 'don't make me want you any more than I do at this moment!'

'Why?' she murmured provocatively, and with a muffled exclamation Damon satisfactorily silenced any further provocation.

CHAPTER THIRTEEN

THAT evening Emma dressed with care for dinner. It was to be Damon's last evening. He was flying back to London the next morning, and while he was there he was going to get a special licence. Then later in the week he would return and they would all go to London for the wedding. Emma only had Johnny to consider and Damon wanted to have the ceremony over before she had time to change her mind again.

But this time Emma had no regrets. Damon needed her, he had proved that ultimately, and she could no longer face life without him. If there were any clouds at all on her horizon they were all connected with Johnny, but Damon could satisfactorily handle him. Johnny had always been a little in awe of the older man, and might respond to a touch of discipline better than she could imagine.

Annabel had taken their news very calmly. It was strange the perception the child had, for when they told her, she said:

'I always thought Daddy had a soft spot for you really, Emma. I mean, he never welcomed your company when I asked for you to come with us, but when you came he always wanted to be with you. I could tell.'

Emma felt her cheeks burn. 'And you don't mind?'

'Of course not. At least . . . I don't think I shall. But if – if you have other children, will I still be the eldest?'

Emma hugged her to her. 'Annabel, you're *our* daughter now, and if we do have any other children then they'll look to you for guidance because you're the eldest, as you say.' She ruffled her hair. 'You said you would like brothers and sisters.'

A shadow crossed Annabel's face. 'But I shan't be able to see them, shall I?'

Emma glanced at Damon. 'Maybe you will,' she said slowly. 'Annabel, I've told your father about what you told me this morning.'

Annabel's sightless eyes sought Damon's. 'Daddy, is that true? Has Emma told you about me leaving you?'

'I already knew, poppet,' replied Damon, taking over from Emma, and lifting Annabel on to his lap.

Annabel pressed her head against his shoulder. 'You know? Oh, Daddy, I was going to do a terrible thing!'

'Don't be silly,' said Damon softly. 'You were only four.'

'I wanted a pony, you see,' murmured Annabel, her eyes a little moist now. 'Elizabeth said she would get me two!' Her voice broke.

'Elizabeth was a strange, unhappy woman,' said Damon quietly, and Annabel hid her face against his neck. Emma left them alone. The groundwork had been done. Now only time might cure her.

So this evening she dressed in a slim-fitting shift of crimson Crimplene, with a low gathered neckline, no sleeves and a straight tunic-like appearance. It suited her to perfection with her dark hair, the straight lines of the dress drawing attention to the curve of her breast, and the long smooth lines of her legs.

Damon was waiting for her in the lounge, seated at the bar, toying with a drink. He rose at her entrance and came towards her. His eyes were warm and caressing, and she marvelled that she had the power to change him so completely, taking the strained look from his face, and making him seem years younger.

He bent to kiss her, and she said: 'I wish you didn't have to go back tomorrow,' in a soft voice.

'So do I,' he replied, releasing her and turning back to the bar. 'What will you drink? A sherry? A cocktail?'

'Sherry, please.' Emma followed him to the bar. 'Is Louisa back?'

'Yes. Tansy tells me she's changing for dinner.' He smiled. 'It's as well she is here. I doubt whether I could leave you alone otherwise.'

Emma flushed prettily, and then turned as Louisa entered the room.

Louisa was dressed in a plain white dress, and looked cool and immaculate.

'Did you have a good day?' asked Emma, seating herself at the bar.

Louisa joined her. 'Very good, thank you.' She smiled. 'I got some lovely material to make myself a suit. I'll show you later.'

Emma studied the drink Damon had slid in front of her, wondering whether Damon intended telling anyone of their changed circumstances. She did not have to wait long.

'I think I should tell you, Emma and I are engaged,' said Damon, offering them both cigarettes.

Louisa's astonishment was apparent. 'This is very sudden!'

'Not really,' said Damon smoothly. 'I first met Emma eight years ago when she worked for the Thorne company in the London office. But . . .' he hesitated, 'but it wasn't until today she agreed to marry me.'

'I see!' Louisa's eyebrows quirked a little. 'Well, what can I say? I hope you'll both be very happy.'

'I'll drink to that,' said Damon, smiling at Emma, and

they raised their glasses.

When dinner was over Louisa tactfully withdrew, leaving Emma and Damon alone together. Damon switched on the stereo radiogram, and soon the cool strains of dance music flooded the room. He switched out the main lights and then seated himself beside her on the low couch where she was dreamily relaxing with a liqueur.

'This is nice,' he murmured, his smile slightly mocking. 'Now, tell me what you've been doing these last seven years. I want to know everything about your life since we were separated.'

Emma shrugged. 'There's very little to tell, actually. After I left Thornes, I went to Saint Benedict's as a student nurse. Eventually I became a staff nurse, and as you know, I was hoping to become a Sister in due time.'

He lit a couple of cigarettes and handed her one. 'Do you miss your work? Do you regret giving it up now?'

Emma snuggled against him. 'No, not really. Oh, to begin with when I first came here I missed the companionship of having cases to talk over, but then somehow it didn't seem to matter any more, and now ... London seems a long way away.' She smiled. 'But I'd not mind being there if you were with me.'

Damon's eyes were warm and caressing as he looked at her. 'Why on earth did you make us waste so much time?' he murmured, his mouth straying gently over her bare arm.

Emma shivered ecstatically. 'Oh, Damon, I'm afraid this won't last. I love you so much. I couldn't bear it if anything happened now.'

'Nothing's going to happen,' he insisted firmly, 'in a week's time we'll be married, and I'll never let you go.'

His mouth found hers passionately. 'I want to teach you what love is; what lovemaking can be like. You have no idea of the intricacies of marriage as yet.'

He smiled, amused when he saw the tell-tale flush sweeping up her tanned cheeks. 'Don't be shy with me,' he said, one hard brown hand smoothing the soft skin of her inner arms. 'I won't hurt you, you know that.'

'I know,' she answered, thinking how very attractive he really was. There was something so essentially male about him, and the dark suits with their narrow trousers which he wore drew attention to the breadth of his shoulders, and the muscular length of his legs.

Suddenly there was a diversion, as footsteps pattered across the hallway and into the lounge. Emma glanced round, and saw Annabel. Immediately she slid out of Damon's arms and crossed the room to the child.

'Annabel!' she exclaimed. 'What are you doing here?'

Annabel looked a little nervous. 'I . . . I wanted to come down and see you two,' she said. 'Something woke me, and I was afraid, and then I remembered that you were going to be my new mummy, so I thought you wouldn't mind if I came down to see you.'

Emma glanced laughingly at Damon. 'Of course we don't mind,' she said soothingly 'But what woke you? Was it Louisa?'

'No.' Annabel shook her head. 'It wasn't Louisa. At least, I'm quite sure it wasn't. I know her way of walking, I can usually tell if it's her.' She hesitated. 'I'm not sure what it was. When I sat up it was quiet, but I thought there was someone there.' She clasped Emma's hand. 'I was afraid, truly. I'm not just saying it.'

Emma drew her over to the couch, and Annabel jumped on to Damon's knee. 'I heard you two talking,' she said, 'so I knew you were here.' She hugged Damon tightly. 'Daddy, you do love Emma, don't you? I mean, you won't find you've changed your mind after . . . after the wedding?'

Emma looked at Damon over Annabel's head, and saw the look in his eyes. It told her more clearly than words that there would be no mistakes this time.

Damon stroked Annabel's hair. 'I love Emma,' he said at last. 'And I won't change my mind. I've loved her for a very long time, so it's very unlikely that I shall ever change now, don't you think?'

'And does Emma love you like that?'

'Of course I do,' said Emma swiftly. 'Don't worry, darling. You're going to have a proper home and family, just like any other little girl, and Daddy and I will always be there when you need us.'

'Oh, I hope so,' said Annabel fervently, and Emma thought how wonderful it would be to make up to the child for all the misery she had experienced, first with her mother, and then with the problems of her condition.

They talked for some time, Annabel opening out completely with her father, telling him about how she was getting on with Louisa, and about Rosa being soon to be a mother again. Emma poured her some lemonade, and she obviously enjoyed being the centre of attraction.

Then, as it grew later, Damon said firmly: 'Time for bed, young lady. It's almost ten o'clock.'

Annabel pulled a face, and Emma thought how unlikely it would be that anyone would actually know she was blind when she was so gay and animated as she was at the moment. Oh, please, she thought intensely, let her see again.

'Will you take me?' Annabel turned to Emma. 'Please.'

Emma lifted her on to the rug. 'Of course. Say good night to your father, and let's go.'

Annabel kissed Damon lovingly, then danced gaily out of the room, followed less exuberantly by Emma.

Emma did not bother to switch on all the lights. The moon illuminated the stairs ahead, and besides, Annabel required no lights to see by.

Surefootedly, Annabel bounced her way upstairs, turning now and again to wait for Emma to catch up with her. She was as carefree as Emma had ever seen her, and that was why Emma did not protest, despite the fact that it seemed unlikely that Annabel would find it easy to sleep after so much excitement.

Her room was in darkness. Annabel had gone ahead, and Emma, a few yards behind, could not see her as she reached the bedroom door. She lifted a hand to switch on the light here, and without warning a hand was pressed against her mouth, successfully preventing the cry of pure astonishment she would have uttered. She was gripped from behind, and the strength of the man's arm and elbow bruised her shoulder and side. She struggled, tugging at his hand with hers futilely, but when the light was flicked on, she saw he held a gun in his other hand, and it was pointing straight at Annabel. The child was crouched beside the bed, at once aware and yet unaware of the danger.

'Emma,' she said falteringly. 'Emma?'

Emma struggled wildly, and then the man spoke. 'What's with this kid? Can't she see you?' He removed his hand. 'One sound, and she's had it!'

Emma rubbed her bruised arm, and ran to Annabel's side, uncaring of the danger. 'Darling,' she whispered, 'it's all right. Just don't make a sound.'

Annabel whimpered, and clung to her, and Emma

took a good look at their intruder. He was short, and thick-set, very black hair, and eyes which did not look wholly European. He wore a thin moustache, and looked a ruthless adversary. He waved the gun now and said:

'Where's Thorne?'

Emma hesitated. 'I . . . I don't know,' she lied.

The man advanced upon her. 'Don't give me that! You've been with him all evening. I've heard you. Where is he? Come on, come on . . . or the kid gets hurt.'

Emma swallowed hard, glancing around. Now that she had had time to notice she could see that this room had been thoroughly searched. It was in a dreadful mess, even the mattress ripped wide open, scattering its filling on the polished wood floor. The playhouse was stripped, its toy tables and chairs tumbled and broken. It was as well Annabel could not see this, she thought.

'He . . . he's in the lounge,' said Emma now, unable to risk Annabel's life for a lie. 'But, please, what do you want? We have no valuables here. For goodness' sake, take whatever you want and go. Just go!'

The man grunted, 'Shut up!'

He turned and glanced along the corridor. All was silence, and as though guessing her thoughts, he said:

'That blonde won't help you, lady, and I don't some-how think anyone else is likely to come rushing to your aid.'

'Louisa? What have you done to her?'

'Nothing, nothing. She's okay.' He grinned maliciously. 'She may have a nasty headache in the morning, but I don't go in for killing dames!'

Emma shook her head. It was like some crazy

nightmare. But she knew there would be no awakening from this. Was this what had awakened Annabel? Surely their lives together were not going to be destroyed before they had begun.

The man waved the gun again. 'Come here,' he said, 'both of you.'

Emma got up slowly. Annabel was trembling and her own legs felt terribly weak. What did he want of them?

'Now,' he said, 'you two lead the way. And don't get any funny ideas, lady, 'cos the kid gets this first, see?'

Emma drew Annabel beside her. 'Come on, darling,' she whispered encouragingly. 'Let's go and find Daddy.'

Annabel squeezed her hand tightly. 'Is ... is this man going to kill my daddy?' Her voice broke on a sob.

Emma shook her head violently. 'No ... No! of course not. He wants to talk to him, that's all.'

'But he has a gun, hasn't he?'

Emma started. 'How do you know that?'

'I guessed. How else would he make us do what he wanted?'

'You've been listening to too much television,' said Emma shakily, but she did not deny it.

The lounge looked warm and inviting in the subdued lights. Damon was on the couch where they had left him, a glass of Scotch in his hand. He was idly flicking through the pages of a motoring magazine, and glanced round in surprise at their entrance.

'Annabel! I thought ... what the hell?' He stopped abruptly, as the man appeared, the small but lethal weapon in his hand.

'Oh, Damon,' Emma whispered, swaying a little, but

160

the man grabbed her arm roughly as Damon leapt to his feet.

'Hold up, lady,' he said. 'Me and Mr. Thorne here have got some bargaining to do.'

CHAPTER FOURTEEN

THE soft balmy air of a warm evening drifted in through the open french doors, scented with perfumes of the flowers that grew in abundance all around the house; mimosa, hibiscus, periwinkle. It was a night for love, for the coming together of lovers lost in the all-enveloping world of their own making. It was certainly not a night for violence, and yet that was what it had turned into.

Emma felt a faint breeze fan her hot forehead, though, despite the heat, she was shivering. Annabel was close beside her as they huddled together on the couch, watching the intruder interrogate Damon. Damon's face was drawn with fatigue; it was five hours since their lives had been disrupted by the arrival of this man and his friends, for there could be no doubt that he had friends assisting him. He would not have come on such a mission alone, they realized that now that the facts had been revealed.

Emma's mind drifted back over all that had been said, remembering the bewildering truth with difficulty. Damon had unknowingly become the pawn in the game, but this man would not believe him.

At first the intruder had been persuasive, asking Damon where the film might be, but as Damon revealed his ignorance he became more violent, threatening Damon with a knife, held in his other hand, while the gun remained menacingly pointed at the girls.

'Mr. Thorne,' he said, his face contorted with anger, 'I am not a patient man. Do not persist in this or you will find I can be very persuasive in an entirely different way. Would you like to see your daughter's face scarred for life? Or perhaps the young lady means more to you.'

Damon had shaken his head, as much in helpless rage as indifference. 'I've told you,' he said, 'I don't know what the hell you're talking about.'

The man lost his temper, bringing the butt of the gun down heavily on Damon's shoulder, throwing him off balance so that he fell, saving himself against the couch. Emma pressed a hand to her mouth to prevent an involuntary cry, and Annabel said:

'What happened? What did he do? Is Daddy hurt?'

'Shut up!' snarled the man, turning on them, and Emma clasped Annabel close against her, trying to protect her if she could.

The man started again, as Damon staggered to his feet, and again Damon denied any knowledge of what he was talking about.

'Look,' said Damon, trying to reason with him. 'Don't you think if I knew anything I would tell you? I don't want my daughter or my fiancée to get hurt.'

The man scoffed. 'Grow up, Thorne. This is common practice for me. I've met dozens of guys like you, and they all think they can get away with that "I'm telling the truth" routine. It won't work! Take my word for it. One way or the other, I'm going to get that film, and when I do . . .'

He came close to Damon, pressing the blade of the knife against his throat. 'Feel that?' he asked. 'Cold, isn't it? Well, that's how you'll all be unless you come to your senses.'

Damon lifted his chin, brushing the sharp blade, and a tiny spurt of blood ran down to his collar. 'Oh, God!'

groaned Emma, feeling sick.

The man took the blade away. It was obvious he had no intention of killing Damon until he told him where the film was. But what film? Emma was puzzled. Was it possible that Damon was working for some government organization without her knowledge? It hardly seemed likely. But stranger things had happened.

The interrogation went on, with Emma and Annabel helpless to help Damon. They were forced to sit and witness Damon's persecution, and for the first time Emma was glad Annabel could not see. It would have hurt her, as it was hurting Emma, to see her father beaten and cuffed, and threatened with a knife, without the power to retaliate because of them.

Once the man knocked Damon unconscious, and uncaring, Emma ran to his side, cradling his head in her lap, and stroking his cheek passionately.

'You swine!' she exclaimed, staring up at the man. 'Why don't you go? Can't you see he doesn't know anything? Can't you see you're only killing him?'

The man wrenched her up, her arm behind her back cruelly. 'Get over there,' he muttered, flinging her across the room. 'Bring me that water siphon.'

Emma rubbed her wrist, and collected the siphon obediently. She thought of turning the siphon on him, but she doubted whether even in his anger he would drop the gun and when it was over one or all of them might be dead. She dared not risk it.

She handed him the siphon, and he turned it on Damon, the cold shock arousing him from unconsciousness. He sat up, a hand to his head, then realizing the circumstances, stood up swiftly, his eyes going first to Emma and Annabel to see whether they were still all right.

And so it went on, until at last, the man said: 'So, my fine friend, we will take the facts, one by one, and then if you can satisfactorily deny them we will see what can be done, yes?'

Damon stared at him tiredly. It was already three o'clock. 'What facts?' he muttered. 'I've told you, I don't know what the hell you're talking about. I'm a businessman, not a spy!'

'It is all the same to me,' said the man, straddling a chair, the gun still pointed menacingly at the girls. 'Whether you are a paid agent, or simply doing this one operation, it is immaterial to me. You will pay for it, one way or the other. And your pretty friends will pay also, unless you decide to tell the truth at last. Until now I have concentrated my persuasive powers on you. Soon it is their turn. I have wasted enough time, but we have all the time in the world. How convenient, Mr. Thorne, that you should live on such a lonely island! It could not be better for our purposes.'

Damon clenched his fists. If he could gain possession of the gun they might have a chance. Even with a gang of them outside the villa, there was the telephone. His eyes must have strayed in that direction for the man said:

'It is dead, Mr. Thorne. Naturally we take all precautions.'

Damon's shoulders sagged. They hadn't a chance. But he wouldn't give up without a fight, if he had an opportunity.

'So,' went on the man. 'Shall I tell you what we know?'

Damon shrugged. 'What can you know? There's nothing to know.'

'Be patient, Mr. Thorne. There is plenty to know.

First of all, can you deny that you knew a very attractive Chinese girl called Tsai Pen Lung?'

Damon's eyes narrowed. He had known it all along, of course. Here was merely confirmation.

'Yes, I knew her,' he said. 'She's dead, isn't she?'

'Unfortunately, yes. A most unhappy affair. She was such a beautiful girl!'

'You killed her?'

'We had to. Unfortunately, as it turned out, she was clean. She had guessed our intention and got rid of the film before she died.'

'Ah, I get it,' muttered Damon. 'You think she passed it on to me. You think I was the contact.'

'We don't *think*, Mr. Thorne. We know. You are the only person she made contact with, and not once, I might add, but several times. It is conceivable that your . . . shall we say . . . charming manner blinded her to the dangers she was running.'

Damon gnawed at his lower lip. 'But don't you see?' he exclaimed. 'If I had been her contact she would have known better than to draw attention to the fact.'

The man frowned. 'That thought had crossed our minds, but it was dismissed again. After all, she was not aware we were on to her at once. And she did go to San Francisco to meet an Englishman.'

Damon stared at him angrily. 'The other killing; was that your doing too? The Englishman?'

'Yes. We thought we had successfully disposed of her contact. It appears we were wrong.'

'But what if you were right?' cried Emma, breaking in on their conversation. 'What if the other man was her contact? Maybe she contacted Damon because she wanted his help. But she didn't get it.'

'My dear young lady, you know nothing about this

affair whatsoever, of that I am certain. After all, Tsai
Pen Lung was a very attractive girl. It is hardly likely
that Mr. Thorne would tell you of his intentions, whatever they might be.'

Emma's cheeks suffused with colour. 'Don't listen to
him, Emma,' muttered Damon imploringly, seeing the
disturbed expression in her eyes.

Emma shook her head, and remained silent.

The man smiled, as though pleased at having found
another method of baiting them. 'So your fiancée did not
know about Tsai Pen Lung,' he said mockingly to
Damon. 'I guessed she would not. Tell me, Mr.
Thorne, did you sleep with her?'

Emma's eyes widened with horror, and Damon felt
an intense hatred assail him. How dared this man insin-
uate such arrant lies in front of Emma, and Annabel. It
was insufferable!

He did not answer the man's question, but the man
apparently decided to return to the matter in hand, for
he went on:

'At some time during your relationship with the girl,
you became her contact. Whether willingly, which I
believe, or unwillingly, it is immaterial. I want that
film!'

'What film? Good God, you've searched here, you've
searched my London apartment; if I had it you would
have found it.'

'Talk sense, Mr. Thorne,' the man ground out furiously. 'This film is minute, a microfilm, no bigger than
that.' He held his forefinger and thumb closely together.
He smiled maliciously. 'Make no mistake about it, Mr.
Thorne. I do not intend to leave here without it.'

Emma gasped, and then went numb again. It could
not be happening; not really. It must be a nightmare.

But it was not. The man kicked the chair away violently, and stood up.

'You have the film, Mr. Thorne. Shall I tell you how I know that? Because our agents in Hong Kong are still safe. If you had already handed the film to the authorities they would have been arrested by now. They would try to escape, naturally, but it would be no good. They would be known. But as yet they are not, so you must have it. When we searched your apartment in London we felt sure we would find it. It was inconceivable that you should leave the country again, taking it with you. That would be too stupid! It had not been handed over, so that was where it must be. But it was not there. We are very thorough, you understand. If it had been there we would have found it. So that leaves you, Mr. Thorne, and this house. But living in the house, I somehow do not think you would leave it lying around. So therefore it must be on your person.' He sighed. 'But this is most unpleasant. I have no desire to search you myself, but if I must, I must.'

'You've already searched me once,' said Damon wearily.

'You think that was a thorough search?'

'What the hell do you mean?'

'Only that the search you have had was superficial. Next time it will be necessary to look everywhere; do you understand, Mr. Thorne? *Everywhere!*' He laughed spitefully. 'I am sure you do not wish these young ladies to witness such indignities. But they will!'

'Oh, God!' Damon bent his head. 'I can't tell you anything else. I don't know where it is. I swear to God, I haven't got it.'

The man shrugged. 'Begin to take off your clothes,

Mr. Thorne.'

Damon shook his head. 'No.'

'I think you will, Mr. Thorne.' He advanced towards Damon slowly. Then he laughed and turned aside, approaching instead the two girls on the settee. He produced the knife and put it tantalizingly close to Emma's throat. 'I think you will, Mr. Thorne,' he repeated, smiling.

Damon clenched his fists until his knuckles were white. With reluctant fingers he unloosened his tie and drew it off slowly. He held it momentarily in his hands weighing his chances. If he did not act now, he would never act at all. What was the use? This man would kill them all anyway. He saw the naked fear on Emma's face, the terrified bundle that was Annabel, and knew he could not let this go on.

With a superhuman lunge, he threw himself across the room at the man, knocking him sideways. He fell across Emma; Annabel screamed and ran wildly across the room.

Damon wrenched him up, off Emma, and saw the knife sticking out of her shoulder where the force of the man's fall across her had plunged it. She was mercifully unconscious, but blood was pouring from her shoulder, causing a brilliant pool of red on the pale rug below.

If anything could have strengthened his resolve it was to see Emma's injury, and to know that unless that wound was staunched soon she would die.

The intruder still had the gun, and the second Damon took in a dazed way to study Emma was sufficient for him to turn it on Damon again. Clasping his hands together Damon brought them down with all the force he could muster on to the man's head before he had time to pull the trigger.

But the man was strong, and he merely grunted furiously like some wild animal, and shaking his head, came on again. Damon closed with him, knowing he hadn't a chance at a distance with the lethal gun in the other man's hand.

They fought savagely, with no holds barred. But although Damon was taller than his adversary, the man was thick-set and muscular, and much more used than Damon to fights of this kind.

He kneed Damon in the stomach, sending him flying back against the far wall, where he slumped, then skidded behind the settee, as a bullet flew past, shattering the window behind him. The standard lamp had turned over and was no use as illumination, but the sun was rising and the room was filling with light.

Damon slid along the floor hastily, before the man had a chance to move, and caught his legs, bringing him down heavily. He fell across him, imprisoning the hand which held the gun against the floor. With his whole weight he gripped the man's wrist, shaking it violently so that the gun fell to the floor sliding across the polished wood to Annabel's feet.

'Annabel,' said Damon grimly, trying to keep the man down with difficulty. 'The gun! It's at your feet; give me the gun!'

Annabel shook her head bewildered. 'Daddy?' she said. 'Daddy? Where are you?'

'Here, here!' said Damon, hanging on for grim death. 'Annabel, get the gun! Hurry, Annabel!'

Annabel bent and lifted the gun with trembling fingers. 'Daddy? Daddy? Where are you?'

'I'm here, darling.' Damon groaned. If only she could see! 'Annabel, here!'

The man was gradually getting free, rolling from under Damon, his hand pressing back Damon's chin. Damon held out a hand helplessly, and to his horror, the man held his hand out too.

If Annabel came too close, she might give the gun to the wrong man. How could she know?

'Annabel,' said Damon desperately, 'be careful. For goodness' sake, don't give it to *him*!'

Annabel stared at them sightlessly, a hand to her mouth, the other hand clutching the gun pitifully.

'How ... how will I know?' she cried tearfully. 'Daddy, where are you?'

She came forward falteringly, and the man lunged forward, grabbing her leg, and throwing her off balance. She fell, hitting her head against the lacquered cabinet of the cocktail bar. Mercifully, the gun fell under her, harmlessly.

Damon brought his fist down on the man's temple, momentarily stunning him, then called:

'Annabel, Annabel! Are you all right?'

The little girl was moving again, scrambling to her feet slowly, lifting the gun again.

'Ye ... yes, I'm all right,' she said dazedly, rubbing her eyes. 'Daddy? Are you still there?'

'Here ... here!' The man was moving again. He must be incredibly strong, thought Damon wearily. 'Annabel, the gun! But don't come too close.'

Annabel moved towards them and circled them warily. She stepped over the tumbled rug and leaning forward put the gun into Damon's hand. With a super-human effort he brought the butt down on the side of the man's head, hitting a vulnerable spot, and with a groan the man slumped unconscious.

His shoulders hunched, Damon got wearily to his

feet, and as he did so two figures appeared in the french door. He stared at them, raising the gun, then saying incredulously:

'Inspector Howard! Good God, man, where did you spring from?'

CHAPTER FIFTEEN

INSPECTOR HOWARD, a loosely-built man in his early fifties, strolled into the room, as casually as though it was any routine call. The sergeant who was with him bent and clipped handcuffs on the man's wrists who was lying unconscious on the floor, clipping them behind his back to prevent any escape.

'Now then, Damon,' he said, crossing to the couch where Emma lay, gradually returning to a pained consciousness. 'What on earth have you been doing? Throwing a wild party?' He grinned, realizing the necessity to release the tension in the room.

Damon slumped, sinking down wearily on to a low chair, his hands, one still holding the gun, hanging loosely between his knees. 'Is she all right?' he asked, looking intently at his friend.

The inspector straightened. 'She's coming round,' he said. 'She's lost a lot of blood. Phillips, go and use the radio on the launch. Send for Doctor Meredith, and tell him to bring transfusion equipment just in case. I don't suppose you know what blood group she is, do you, Damon?'

Damon shook his head, and the sergeant nodded to his superior and went out. 'She'll be okay,' said the inspector. 'How about you? And you, too, little Annabella?'

Annabel was standing, leaning against the back of her father's chair, a wild, strained look in her eyes. She did not answer the inspector and her father swung round.

'Annabel,' he murmured. 'Honey, are you all right?'

Annabel shook her head. 'Daddy,' she said faintly. 'Didn't you notice? I gave *you* the gun.'

Damon sprang up, his weariness evaporating. 'Annabel!' he exclaimed. 'So you did! Can you *see*!' He was incredulous.

Emma, hearing his words, propped herself up, too. 'Can you?' she asked weakly. 'Annabel, can you really?'

Annabel gripped the chair very tightly. 'Well . . . I'm beginning to, I think,' she said, tears streaming down her cheeks. 'I . . . I can't see clearly. It's all blurred, but I could tell which was you, Daddy. I *had* to, didn't I?'

Damon pulled her to him, hugging her closely. 'Oh, Annabel,' he said, almost choking with emotion. 'Annabel!'

Annabel hugged him, and then, watched intently by Damon and the inspector, she made her way slowly to Emma on the couch. Emma slumped back, unable to hold up any longer, and Annabel bent over her, burying her face in her neck. 'Oh, Emma,' she whispered, 'I'm going to see again, aren't I?'

Damon thought tiredly that it was worth the night of terror if it meant that Annabel should see again. It might take time, but the blockage had been broken, and the first light could be seen.

He went down on his knees beside the couch when Annabel drew back, and said:

'Darling Emma, are you really all right?'

Emma squeezed his hand tightly. 'I will be. It's only a little painful. I've got to be, haven't I? There's so much to look forward to.'

Damon kissed her hand gently, and then rose to his feet again.

'And now,' he said, turning to the inspector, 'explanations, please. Why are you here? And what about that man's accomplices?'

'He had only one accomplice,' replied Inspector Howard, 'and we dealt with him on the beach.'

'I see. But how do you come to be here? I mean, how could you know?'

'We didn't. Oh, at least, we've known these two were in Nassau since their plane landed, but naturally we didn't connect them with you. Why should we? But they've been kept under surveillance, just the same. No, Damon, it wasn't them who brought us here, although we heard a shot as we neared the island, and knew something was up. It was your nurse, a Miss Emma Harding. Is she here?'

Damon's eyes narrowed. 'I'm Emma Harding,' said Emma, her cheeks paler than ever. 'What do you want me for?'

The inspector's eyes darkened. 'But I thought . . . I mean . . .' he looked helplessly at Damon. 'From your attitude I naturally assumed that this young lady was . . . well . . .'

'She is my fiancée,' replied Damon coolly. 'We're being married at the end of the week. Why?'

'I see.' The inspector nodded. 'How very unfortunate!'

Emma gasped as she fell back suddenly, a hand to her shoulder. She had passed out again.

'Oh, God!' said Damon, crossing swiftly to her side. 'Do you think I should try and take her to the mainland?'

'No. Don't move her. You would only do her more harm than good.'

The sergeant returned at that moment before any more could be said. 'The doctor's on his way,' he said, in answer to their questioning glances. 'He's coming from Aldoro. He should be here in twenty minutes.'

'Thank heaven', said Damon fervently. 'But, Bob,' he turned to the inspector, 'what's happened? What do you want Emma for?'

The inspector frowned. 'Unfortunately, in the circumstances, which you, my friend, have yet to explain, I have some bad news for her. It would be as well if we discussed this matter elsewhere, in case she should regain consciousness and overhear our conversation.'

Damon heard footsteps outside, and said: 'Good lord, Louisa, and the rest of the household. No one has been to see if they're all right.'

'Sergeant.' Inspector Howard indicated that Phillips should go and investigate, while Tansy, the old housekeeper, appeared in the doorway

'Why, Mr. Thorne,' she exclaimed. 'What on earth is going on?'

Damon shook his head wearily. 'I'll explain later, Tansy,' he said. 'Are you all right? Has anyone been to your room?'

'Not that I know of. Why? Has there been trouble?' She saw the body on the floor and gasped, 'Lord help us, what's going on?'

'Later, Tansy, later,' said Damon impatiently. 'Look. Emma has been injured. The doctor is on his way. Could you stay here with her while I speak to the Inspector in private?'

'Of course, of course.' Tansy hurried across the room to Emma's side. 'Och, the poor child! And Annabel, my love, are you feeling all right? No one has harmed you, have they?'

Annabel danced up and down, excitement vying with the feeling of frightened helplessness which was gradually evaporating. Damon and the inspector left her telling Tansy her good news.

In Damon's study he turned to his friend impatiently. 'What bad news?' he asked.

'She had a brother, is that right? John Harding?'

'*Had* a brother?'

'I'm afraid so. Did you know, by the way, that he'd stolen over two hundred pounds from your company?'

'A while ago, yes,' Damon nodded. 'That's being dealt with.'

'No, during the last couple of months. It's the usual story – debts he couldn't pay, threatened by thugs hired by the bosses of these gambling clubs to collect their debts for them.'

'And?' Damon's eyes had narrowed.

'Apparently he wrote to his sister, asking her to send him authority to draw some money from her bank. Your ... er ... fiancée sent him that authority, but it wasn't enough. The night before last he was involved in a car chase through the streets of London; whether intentionally or unintentionally we shall never know, but he crashed. He was killed instantly. The London police traced his nearest relative to your household.'

'I see.' Damon ran a tired hand over his forehead. 'What a business! But I don't think she ought to be told right now. She's been through enough tonight.'

'I agree,' the inspector nodded. 'Come, we'd better return to your housekeeper. I should hate that man to come round and attack her.'

Phillips had returned when they got back to the lounge. He told them that as only Louisa Meredith slept in this part of the house, apart from Damon, Annabel and Emma of course, she had been the only one disturbed. She had been knocked unconscious, but was recovering now and would likely be examined by Doctor Meredith on his arrival.

Emma was only half conscious now, and Damon swore angrily.

'Where the devil is Meredith?' he stormed, striding about the room. 'Doesn't he know this is an emergency?'

Inspector Howard regarded him compassionately. 'Damon,' he said, 'let's try and pass the time by considering the circumstances which led up to this situation. Why were these men here? What was their motive for attacking you?'

Slowly, and methodically, Damon gave the inspector the whole story, from the time he first saw Tsai Pen Lung in Hong Kong Airport. He told him about the killings in San Francisco, and the ultimate search of his apartment. Finally he described the night which had just passed.

Sergeant Phillips had written it all down, and the inspector frowned thoughtfully.

'It's very strange,' he said, 'that you should be contacted by the girl if you weren't involved. Myself, like these men, I would surmise that you'd agreed to act as contact, after the death of this other Englishman.' He drew out his cigarette case. 'You must see, Damon, that your actions have been such as to arouse suspicion. After all, your home is here, yet you return directly to London after leaving San Francisco.'

'I'm a businessman,' exclaimed Damon wearily. 'I go where I have to. Besides, if I'd been the contact, why didn't I leave the film, if there is such a thing, in London?'

The inspector shrugged. 'Oh, there'll be such a

thing,' he said definitely. 'It's possible that you might be considering putting the film up for auction. It has been known.'

'You mean . . . to different governments?'

'Exactly. I can imagine several heads of state who would like to read what's on that film.'

'Bob! Do you honestly think I might *really* have the film?' Damon was aghast.

Inspector Howard shook his head. 'No, Damon, I don't. I've known you too many years to be able to believe that you would willingly put Miss Harding and your daughter's life in danger for the sake of something like this. Besides, you're not that kind of man.'

'Thank God for that!' muttered Damon fervently.

Footsteps outside heralded the arrival of the doctor. Damon breathed a sigh of relief, and while Doctor Meredith examined Emma, two stalwart police officers who had arrived with the doctor removed the recovering body of the intruder from the floor of the lounge.

Things were gradually returning to normal. Tansy took Annabel away and tucked her up in bed where Doctor Meredith would examine her in due course, while after an injection and treatment for her shoulder, Emma was carried upstairs by Sergeant Phillips and put to bed. Damon had wanted to carry her up, but the inspector had detained him, asking more questions, and stating that Damon was in no fit state to carry anyone around.

After the room had been emptied, Damon sank down exhaustedly on the couch.

'Not long now,' said the inspector, patting his shoulder. 'I'm sorry to plague you like this, but getting rid of those two is not the end of the affair. So long as they think you have the film you're in danger, so somehow between us we've got to make sure you haven't, and if you haven't, where is it?'

Damon shook his head. 'Hell, Bob, don't you think I want to know that? I'm heartily sick of the whole affair, and I want out!'

'Well, you can't get out, without some difficulty,' remarked the inspector. 'Once this film is in the authorities' hands, you're a free man, but until then . . .'

'. . . I'm to be hounded!' muttered Damon glumly. 'I need a drink!'

Inspector Howard poured him a stiff whisky and handed it to him. Damon gulped it thirstily, and the inspector poured him another. Damon felt around for his cigarettes, sliding one into his mouth, and producing his lighter automatically.

Then, like a flash of lightning, a thought struck him.

'I've had an idea,' he exclaimed, getting to his feet a little unsteadily.

'Well, steady on,' said Inspector Howard. 'Think calmly!'

'I can't. God, why didn't I think of it before?'

The inspector sighed. 'Think of what?'

'Well, whenever I've thought of Tsai, it's always been about the times I was with her, and then I knew she'd run out on me because she was frightened. But there's something else I forgot. When we were in this bar in Frisco, she borrowed my lighter; this lighter. Then, when she got frightened, as I told you, she disappeared, but she took my lighter with her. At first I thought she'd stolen it, but when we went out of the bar, the manager of the hotel gave me the lighter back again, and I thought no more about it. I knew by then she'd left, of course, and I naturally assumed she'd just returned my lighter as an afterthought. Don't you see? That might be the link?'

The inspector looked interested. 'It might indeed. Damon, why didn't you think of this before?'

'It's like I told you. It never really seemed important. But now I see it was the most important thing of all.'

The inspector took the lighter from him swiftly, flicking it expertly. It lit at once, and there was obviously nothing wrong with its mechanics.

'The filling,' said the inspector, rapidly unscrewing the pin at the bottom. With cool precision he drew out the cottonwool from the tiny hole, and Damon envied him his control.

He emptied the contents on to the glass top of a coffee table, and suddenly there it was – a minute roll of film, embedded in cottonwool.

'Excellent,' said Inspector Howard, with a mocking smile. 'I shall expect promotion for this!'

Damon smiled also, unable to believe it was all over. 'You deserve it, Chief Inspector,' he muttered, lighting his cigarette with a match from a box on the table. 'What a night, *what* a night!'

CHAPTER SIXTEEN

EXACTLY one month later Emma carried a tray of tea into her husband's bedroom at their London apartment. She was wearing a dark blue silk dressing gown which moulded the full curves of her slim body. With a blue hairband securing the swathe of dark hair, she looked about eighteen, thought Damon, as he lay lazily watching her approach. Although she had been his wife for two whole weeks he still had not lost that thrill of possession he had first felt when he slid the broad gold band on her finger.

And they were happy, as he had known they would be, and she was everything he had ever wanted in a woman. She had lost now that faint air of nervousness she had shown the first night they were together, when she had been half afraid to release her emotions fully. But gradually he had taught her how to please him and in so doing had opened up a whole new exciting world for herself. Now she was completely uninhibited with him, as eager as he was to climb the heights of passion. He could still make the hot colour flood her cheeks if ever he gently mocked her, but she was getting to know him all the time so that she knew when he was teasing her, and could retaliate in kind.

Now she placed the tea tray on a low table beside the bed, and said:

'Did I waken you?'

'Hm, what time is it?'

Emma lifted his watch off the dressing table. 'Almost eight,' she replied, replacing it. 'Do you want some tea?'

Damon grinned. 'Do you?'

'Yes.' Emma poured herself a cup, adding milk and sugar. Then seating herself in a low armchair at the foot of the bed she sipped it, eyeing him covertly over the rim of the cup.

Damon shrugged, and leaning over poured himself a cup too, which he drank in two mouthfuls. 'There,' he remarked mockingly. 'Thank you.'

Emma smiled. 'Well,' she said defensively, 'I was thirsty.'

'Come here,' he said.

Emma continued to sip her tea, ignoring him.

'Come here,' he repeated commandingly.

Emma shook her head. 'I want to finish my tea.'

It was a delicious excitement to torment him like this, for she knew what form her punishment would take. Damon's eyes had darkened, and she thought how utterly he held her in thrall. She knew every line of his hard body, had known what it was like to hold him trembling with passion in her arms. She loved him completely, and could not bear now the thought of life without him.

She finished her tea, and rose to her feet, stretching lazily. Damon rolled on to his stomach and closed his eyes. Emma compressed her lips.

'Damon,' she said tentatively. 'Damon!'

'Mmn?' he grunted, and Emma kicked off her slippers angrily.

Then she walked to the bed, and pulled him round to face her. He did not touch her, allowing her to make all the running. 'Damon,' she said appealingly, 'don't be cross with me.'

Damon smiled lazily. 'I'm not cross,' he replied. 'Go and get dressed. I'm not getting up yet.'

'Oh, *you*!' Emma stamped her foot with rage, and he laughed.

'Temper, temper,' he said mockingly, and then, unable to tease her any longer, pulled her down to him, kicking aside the silk coverings of the bed so that she was close against the muscular warmth of his body.

'Damon,' she whispered achingly, 'what if someone should come in?'

'You're my wife, aren't you?' he murmured thickly, his mouth satisfactorily silencing any further protest she might have felt it her duty to make.

Much, much later Emma reluctantly roused herself, looking down on Damon with adoring eyes. He smiled.

'Are you happy?' he asked, carrying the palm of her hand to his mouth.

'Need you ask?' she said, sliding her arms back into the sleeves of her dressing gown. 'I've never been so happy before. You know that.'

'And Johnny?' he said deliberately. They had not talked much about her brother since the funeral.

Emma sighed. 'Oh, darling, you know I miss him sometimes. But I can't help but be grateful that the inspector came to tell us about him at that particular moment. Had he not arrived, I don't know what would have happened.'

'No,' agreed Damon seriously. 'It was lucky that Bob came so early. He thought I might be using my time in sailing while I was home, and he knows I like to get away early in the morning.'

'It was very lucky,' said Emma, closing her eyes for a moment, reliving those hours of horror. She shivered. 'Poor Johnny! To be killed like that, with the hounds after you! It's an awful thought!'

Damon sighed. 'I wonder sometimes whether it would have happened had I not forced you to go to Sainte Dominique.'

'But that's ridiculous!' exclaimed Emma, shaking her head. 'Johnny has been in and out of trouble as long as I can remember. He was always wanting money. Sooner or later the time was bound to come when his debts exceeded his assets.'

Damon looked intently at her. 'Is that what you seriously believe?'

Emma frowned. 'Of course. Why? Did you think I might blame you?'

'The thought had crossed my mind,' he confessed, shrugging.

'Oh, Damon,' she whispered, and then slid determinedly off the bed. 'I must get dressed. Annabel will be up soon.'

Damon smiled. 'All right.'

She looked back at him suddenly. 'By the way, I wanted to ask before but didn't like to, did you sleep with that Chinese girl?'

Damon stared at her in astonishment, and then slid forcefully out of bed, pulling on his own silk dressing gown. He caught her by the door, pinning her there with his arms.

'Emma Thorne!' he muttered, with mock-derision, 'how dare you even ask such a thing?'

Emma flushed, her new-found temerity vanishing.

'Well . . . I . . . I only wondered,' she said hotly.

Damon's eyes softened. 'Okay, okay,' he said. 'I'll forgive you.'

'And?'

He shook his head. 'Of course not. I've never even looked at another woman since you came to my office to

185

ask me to help Johnny.'

'Oh, thank you, darling,' she murmured, hugging him close. 'And now I can get my bath in peace.' She turned. 'By the way, yesterday Annabel read the first page of her new book, and Doctor McAndrew thinks it will only be a matter of time before her eyes are completely adjusted again.'

Damon smiled. 'We're very lucky, aren't we, Emma?'

'And contented, too,' said Emma, looking back at him lovingly, before she walked confidently through the door into the bathroom.

Experience the warmth of...

Harlequin Romance

**The original romance novels.
Best-sellers for more than 30 years.**

Delightful and intriguing love stories
by the world's foremost writers
of romance fiction.

Be whisked away to dazzling
international capitals...
or quaint European villages.
Experience the joys of falling in love...
for the first time, the best time!

Harlequin Romance

**A uniquely absorbing journey
into a world of superb romance reading.**

**No one touches the heart of a woman
quite like Harlequin!**

What readers say about Harlequin romance fiction...

"Harlequin romances give me a whole new outlook on life."
S.P.,* Mecosta, Michigan

"Thank you so much for all those lovely hours of entertainment."
K.Z., Whiting, New Jersey

"Harlequin is the best in romantic reading."
K.G., Philadelphia, Pennsylvania

"Thank you very much for letting me subscribe to Harlequin romances."
M.J.B., Hendersonville, North Carolina

"A pleasant way to relax after a busy day."
P.W., Rector, Arkansas

*Names available on request.

Harlequin Presents...

The very finest in romantic fiction

Get all the latest books before they're sold out!

As a Harlequin subscriber you actually receive your personal copies of the latest Presents novels immediately after they come off the press, so you're sure of getting all 6 each month.

Cancel your subscription whenever you wish!

You don't have to buy any minimum number of books. Whenever you decide to stop your subscription just let us know and we'll cancel all further shipments.

Your FREE gift includes

Sweet Revenge by **Anne Mather**
Devil in a Silver Room by **Violet Winspear**
Gates of Steel by **Anne Hampson**
No Quarter Asked by **Janet Dailey**